The Amplified
by Lauren M. Flauding

Chapter 1

My brother would make fun of me.

I picture his playful yet condescending expression and manage a smile despite my labored breathing. I run in time to the music coming from my ancient device, pushed along by the rhythm that is so seldom found in our current songs. I try to decide which offense he would attack first.

"Mari, why do you use that *relic* to listen to music? The Adhesives are so much easier and you don't have to *carry* anything..."

True, the Adhesives are easier. One small patch placed on my temple allows me to listen to an hour of music or watch a movie without the hindrance of wires, attachments, or receivers. But I don't care much for the Adhesives. Once, my friend Alia made me adhere some awful movie about cat-people in love, and I couldn't make it stop. I just had to let it play through my auditory and optical systems until it ended and the patch dissolved into my skin. I much prefer seeing movies on our old holograph machine.

I pass the school, noting with some satisfaction that I'm just now starting to feel the burn in my legs. Some of the students are having their outside hour. Even from far away I can tell that it's the older ones, probably 11 or 12-year-olds, lounging on the play equipment and chatting with each other. Younger students would be running around, playing games, and generally expending the energy not yet stifled by years of absorbing information.

I run a little faster to get the school out of my view. I'm glad that I finished all my curriculum last year, trading in the endless barrage of images, educational films and holographic lectures from the Governor for a few months of labor before going away for training. A lot of 15-year-olds complain about the labor. The tasks in the factories and on the farms are a lot more physically demanding than the lethargy of school, but I welcome the change. Plus, it's nice spending time with my mother when we harvest.

I've left the paved streets of our compound, and now my feet thump on the welcome expanse of soft dirt. I take in the landscape, so dry and vast, stretching out for miles with the occasional jagged hill jutting out defiantly to break up the flatness. I suppose it's a good reminder that even though we're all trying to be the same, there are still some of us that stick out. Sometimes it really is incredible to think that we've managed to survive in this environment for so long; a feat that likely would not have been possible without the Amplifiers.

I try to hold my breath as I run through a cloud of dust, but some particles find their way into my nose and I choke anyway. I dig into the pocket of my shorts to find my Hydration capsule and swallow it between coughing fits. Immediately the dryness in my throat subsides and I feel the simulated liquid spreading throughout my body. I'm glad, I need the energy I lost from hacking the dirt out of my lungs.

Peering ahead, I see the culprit of the dust cloud; that huge, stupid, Mall-cruiser. I never take it to the city if I can help it. I guess the arenas, capsule bars and sleeping pods would seem like an attractive way to travel for some people, but to me it just seems dull; lumbering along at a snail's pace, watching everyone try to entertain themselves. It's for people who like to waste time. And I rarely have time to waste.

I'm running parallel to the Mall-cruiser in no time, and I hear some children shouting insults out the open windows.

"Where are you running to, chicken legs?"

"Hope you're racing off to find a shower, you dirty *clam*!"

I put on my most menacing face and sprint right up to the windows. The children scream and cower beneath the glass, their insolence now completely extinguished in their fear. I beat on the panes a few times for good measure, and hear some strangled yelps as I pull away. I would laugh if it didn't throw off my breathing pattern, so instead I settle for a feeling of smug satisfaction.

I can just see the outline of the city, the towering center of what some call our spider Community. From the air barges, you would be able to see the Mall-cruiser tracks stretching out like skinny legs from the metropolis to the surrounding eight compounds, all labeled by one letter of the word 'equality.' I remember seeing all the images of the compounds in school. They all looked pretty much the same, but when the image of our compound, Compound Q, would come up, somehow we

7

recognized it, and we would all cheer. It seems an odd thing to have done, especially now that I'm feeling less and less attached to my compound.

Reaching the city limits, I glance up at the massive clock looming over the old hospital. 11:37. Right on time. The soldiers should be arriving in a few minutes. I run past the control tower and blow a kiss to the guards stationed there. They don't react, as always. Stoic expressions and rigid posture are characteristic of this post. Once, when we were younger, my brother and I put hats and sunglasses on the tower guards. They didn't move. But it was a particularly hot day so I think they might have been grateful. Luckily, nobody has to stay in that position for too long at a time. The motionless guards there today might be foremen at the factories or entertainers at the clubs next week, depending or their work rotation. Everyone alternates their labor positions. Except the Restrainers, of course.

With the landing park in sight, I sprint the last hundred yards or so and collapse on a bench near the waiting zone. I breathe heavily and people stare at me, but I'm used to it. I already stand out among the workers in my T-shirt and shorts, but it's also unusual to see anyone in the city exert themselves. Or sweat. I stretch out my legs and slump back on the bench, closing my eyes and turning my face to the sun. It's a beautiful day, my brother is returning from Service, and in a couple weeks I'll be Amplified.

Life is good.

Chapter 2

I'm alarmed by the sudden darkness until I open my eyes and realize the air barge is flying overhead. The barge is about as big as the city and completely shuts out the sun. It takes a while for my eyes to adjust, but soon I can see them. Soldiers jump off the edge of the barge and plummet toward the ground. The sirens come on to clear the landing park, but there's really no need. Anytime an air barge flies over, the slick, grated floor of the park is immediately vacated.

I crane my neck and watch in awe as the soldiers fall, some performing intricate acrobatics as they fly through the air. As they near the landing park, the turbines start to whir, forcing massive gusts of air through the grates and sending errant pieces of trash left in the park shooting into the sky. If I watch closely, I can see the point where the turbines take effect. There's a slight jerk as the soldiers hit the turbine's threshold, which begins the slowing of their descent.

I've watched people land in the park dozens of times, but it still fascinates me. The smallest movement of a hand or a foot sends them sailing or spiraling in a different direction. Soon, they're all hovering about 40 yards up in the air where the force of the turbines hold them safely. Finally, the great machines power down and the soldiers, almost in unison, float toward the ground.

The siren ceases and all of us in the waiting zone quickly step forward into the park. There aren't many people greeting the returned soldiers. I suspect most of their family and friends are still traveling here on the Mall-cruiser. I search for my brother among all the unfamiliar faces. Somehow, all the soldiers look the same; immaculately fit young women and men, dressed in the same gray uniforms, carrying themselves with the confidence characteristic of the Amplified. It's hard to believe they're all only nineteen years old.

How am I going to recognize him? I think. *It's been almost four years.* The last time I saw my brother was in the week-long break between his Training and the beginning of his Service. He spent almost the entire time running up the walls, jumping off the roof, and generally scaring my poor mother to death. It was incredible. From that time on, I became obsessed with Amplification.

I turn around and accidentally run into a tall female soldier.

"Watch where you're going, little girl!" She yells condescendingly. I feel my cheeks get hot, but I manage to mumble an apology before turning away. *Little girl? I'm fifteen years old!* But as I look at the hundreds of impressive soldiers around me, I realize how small I feel.

I'm starting to get frustrated, wondering now if I should have just stayed at home and waited for my brother to get there. At this point, he may have already started heading out of the city. I catch a glimpse of a face that could belong to my brother. I start heading in that direction when I hear someone behind me.

"Mari?"

"Adrian! Wait... Adrian?"

I turn and see the biggest version of my brother I could have ever imagined. He has my brother's dark hair and mischievous smile, but in the place of his once-lanky physique are bulging muscles. His young, 19-year old face looks out of place above his thick neck. But before I can fully process his transformation, he's enveloped me with his massive arms and pulled me off the ground. I suppose this is what people mean by a "bear hug."

"Hey little sis!" He bellows in my ear, his voice markedly deeper. "You haven't changed a bit!"

"Sure I have! Maybe not as much as *you*… what did you do, swallow a lion?"

Adrian chuckles as he sets me back down on the ground. He glances down at his body, clearly pleased with himself, but still attempts to be modest.

"Something like that. Just a lot of Protein and compulsory weight training."

I don't know what he means by "Protein," it must have something to do with the different capsules they ingest during Service.

"Well, it's good to see you again ... all of you," I say as I stand back and look at my brother one more time. "Come on, let's get home. Mom and Daniel are so excited that you're back!"

"I'm excited to see them," Adrian admits. We've started walking out of the landing park. "What's Daniel like now? I guess he's grown up a lot, huh?"

"Yeah, he's a fireball. Quite the independent 8-year old," I respond. "Oh, you won't believe this! Last week he took all of the blankets and camped out-"

11

"When does the next Mall-cruiser get here?" Adrain interrupts.

"Mall-cruiser? I don't know, I thought we'd just run home."

"Run? Are you kidding? How far is that?"

"About twelve miles. It's not a big deal, I ran here."

"Sounds like torture."

"Well, sometimes it is, but then I just feel that much better when I'm done."

Adrian gives me an exasperated look, an expression that I remember from countless arguments similar to this one.

"Mari, why do you try so hard?"

"Because I'm not content to sit around and do nothing until I get Amplified."

Adrain smiles and shakes his head.

"I guess you really haven't changed much, have you?"

"Guess not."

———-

After a lot of coercion, Adrian finally persuades me to take the Mall-cruiser with him. It's full of returned soldiers and their families, as well as a bunch of loiterers who are probably in the free week of their work rotation. Several girls eye my brother as we pass. I glance at him and see that he's smiling. Maybe this is why he wanted to ride the Mall-cruiser, more opportunities to show off his rippling muscles. Or maybe it's the arenas; the huge, dome-like rooms where the Amplified challenge each other. My brother looks wistfully at the closed doors, but he wouldn't leave me alone. It's not a written rule that only the Amplified are allowed in the arenas, because that would be in violation of the Equality Movement, but everyone knows that's how it is anyway. There are no windows, but from the cheering, thumping, and occasional bloodcurdling scream, I can imagine what's going on in there.

We end up in one of the many capsule bars. This one has some kind of tacky jungle theme. We weave through fake vines and sit down at a small table. A bored-looking waiter dutifully approaches us and holds out his Transcriber. We each place our hands on the screen, and the waiter reads out our information.

"Quillen, Marianna." I flinch at the sound of my full name. "Age 15. Not Amplified. Approved for all non-intoxicating capsules." I bristle even more. I don't need some stupid electronic menu reminding me of my Amplification status. The waiter turns to my brother.

"Quillen, Adrian. Age 19. Amplified. Approved for all capsules."

"Great," Adrian replies. "I'll have a Twisted Shark Bait."

I roll my eyes. Leave it to my brother to order one of the fancy capsules. The waiter eyes me expectantly.

"I'll just have a Hydration."

"Which flavor?"

Which flavor? It really has been a long time since I've been on this stupid cruiser.

"Uh, just regular."

The waiter sighs. Apparently I've just made his job as mundane as possible. "Please note that these will be taken out of your weekly rations."

The waiter leaves and I turn back to Adrian. I have thousands of questions.

"So tell me about the last 4 years! How was your Service?"

Adrian's eyes light up as he leans forward.

"Oh man, Mari, Amplification really is as amazing as everyone says. I mean, you can do anything! The Service itself was actually pretty lame, mostly guarding the prisons and tagging animals. The only exciting part was when we battled the Dissenters."

Normally, mention of a battle would make me nervous. But I remember the images of the Dissenters from school; dull, idiotic-looking people with missing teeth, brandishing their primitive weapons. The battles are hardly fair, with the Dissenters being so thoroughly outmatched, but they keep persisting. I still wonder why anyone would want to get rid of the Amplifiers. Seems like the best thing in the world to me.

"Last year, there was a group of Dissenters trying to infiltrate the Activation Base," Adrian continues, "and we had them surrounded before they even crossed the perimeter. But then one of them-"

Adrian's story is interrupted by a burst of yelling and a loud cracking sound from across the bar. A large soldier has just thrown an older man, probably about 65 years old, onto a table, splitting it in two. The soldier rushes at the man again, his victim trying to scramble away from the wreckage of the table, but he's too slow. The soldier gives himself an unintelligible command and grabs the older man by the ankles, swinging him around while screaming:

"You wanna bet against Amplification again, old man?"

The soldier finally swings the older man up above his head with astonishing strength, then slams him to the ground. The old man moans as the soldier steps over him and walks out of the bar.

Horrified, I rush over to the man crumpled on the floor. He has a few scrapes, and his leg is curled at an irregular angle.

"Adrian, help him!" I plead.

"Ah, he probably deserved it."

I stare at him in disbelief, trying to figure out if he's joking. He stands with his arms folded across his chest, looking unconcerned.

"Adrian!" I hiss, willing my brother to snap out of his indifference.

"Fine," he concedes reluctantly and kneels down beside the man. "Adrian, asses the victim's injuries," he commands himself. I can see my brother's body relax as the Amplifier takes over. He moves his hands expertly over the man's body, pausing at a few areas. Adrian addresses the old man.

"Sir, your hip has been dislocated. Would you like me to fix it?"

"Yes!" The man wheezes pitifully. "Please."

Adrian grimaces and again accesses his Amplifier. "Adrian, reset the joint."

He slowly pulls the man's knee up and rocks it back and forth, then quickly jerks the entire upper leg away from the floor, causing a satisfying popping sound. The old man exhales, clearly relieved of the worst of his pain. He looks over at Adrian.

"Thank you for helping me, thank you so much." He murmurs over and over. Adrian doesn't respond, doesn't even look at the man. He just stands and walks away.

———-

"What was that all about?" I mutter to Adrian once I catch up with him outside the bar.

"What?" He answers innocently.

"Oh, so I guess I'm supposed to believe you're always a selfish, unwilling jerk?"

Adrian's face hardens and he pulls me into the nearest vacant sleeping pod.

"It's just that… the guy wasn't Amplified."

"Neither is mom, are you gonna leave her for dead when someone attacks her too?"

"No! It's different with mom, I just..." He trails off, realizing he has no solid argument. After a long pause he looks up at me, but doesn't meet my eyes. "Four years in the Service will make you think differently about certain people, ok?"

No, I think, *It's not ok*. I sit down on the small bed and think about the years of taunts and bullying I endured because I was the child of a *clam*, a stupid nickname for people who aren't Amplified. Those early years of trying to fight off several kids at one time, often kids that were a lot bigger than me. With no adults at the school, it was easy for them to get away with stuff like that. The closest thing to authority were the cameras mounted everywhere, but we didn't know if anyone was watching on the other end, or if they even cared.

Our teachers at school were the images, the projections, and the occasional holographic appearance of the Governor. My classmates used to say that if you walked through the hologram of Governor Plenaris, you would die. So one day I walked up and stuck my hand into the edge of the hologram. I didn't die, but it seared off the tip of my right index finger. It was incredibly painful, but I just went back to my seat, determined not to cry or show any weakness. That was the day the kids at my school stopped bothering me.

I rub the shortened tip of that finger as I stare out the tiny window of the sleeping pod. Adrian is leaning against the wall with his eyes closed, but I know he's not asleep. I wonder what other changes he might have made underneath all those new muscles, what kinds of experiences drove him to share the same sentiments as people who shout insults at strangers from the Mall-cruiser and beat up defenseless old men in bars. Will I come back with those opinions after my four years of Service?

"Hey Mari," Adrian murmurs, his eyes still closed, "do you remember when we used to mess with the control tower guards?"

I smile in spite of myself.

"Yeah, those were good times."

———-

As soon as we turn the corner onto our street, I see my younger brother Daniel jump up from our front porch and start bounding toward us.

"A-A-Adrain!" He yells in that heartbreaking stutter. It's actually kind of endearing. I'm not really looking forward to his Amplification when he'll likely find a way to fix it. Daniel slams right into Adrian and wraps his arms around his older brother's trunk-like legs. Adrian reaches down to tousle Daniel's stick-straight brown hair. They marvel at one another's transformations as they approach the house. I see Adrian's playful expression change when he sees our mother leaning against the doorframe.

She is still a beautiful woman. Age and worry have etched a few lines into her tan skin and woven some gray streaks into her long, dark hair, but I've noticed the way some of the men at the farm look at her. I know she can always feel their stares.

She opens her arms wide as we approach, her vacant eyes searching the air in front of her.

"Where is my first born?" She jokes lightly, smiling as see waits expectantly.

"Right here, mom," Adrian replies, moving into her embrace.

"Adrian!" My mother exclaims. "You left here a boy and came back a ... bear!" She feels his arms, shoulders, and face, letting her hands see what her eyes cannot.

"Ah, mom, it's not a big deal," Adrian dodges sheepishly.

"Yes it is!" Daniel pipes up. "He's three t-times the size he w-w-was when he left!"

I notice Adrian is actually starting to feel self-conscious, so I change the subject.

"Hey, all of Adrian's belongings from Service arrived this morning, right?"

Daniel lights up.

"That's right! I've been d-dying to go through them but mom m-made me wait!" He ducks into the house, pulling Adrian in with him. "C-c-come on, Adrian, you've g-g-g-got to show m-me everything!"

Mom sighs as her sons pass by. I take her elbow to lead her into the house, even though she rarely needs guidance.

"He's changed," she remarks.

"Yeah, he's gotten big."

"Hm. That too."

I always marvel at how much my mother can see in spite of her blindness.

Chapter 3

"Ugh! These stupid worms keep getting in the way!" My friend Alia wrinkles her nose as she flings another poor worm over the fence.

"They're not that bad," I tease. "I think they're kind of cute."

"Then why don't you take some of them home as pets so I don't have to keep feeling them squish between my fingers!"

I can't help but smile. With her delicate skin and glowing blonde hair, Alia looks more likely to be a movie star than someone sitting in the dirt pulling up weeds.

"I wish Joby were here," Alia pouts, "then I wouldn't be the only one complaining."

I laugh as I imagine our friend Joby, who might be the laziest person I know, continuously bending over and digging around in the dirt with the hot sun on his back. Luckily for him, he got his labor assignment in the nutrition factory, sitting all day sorting through small machinery parts.

"Calm down, Alia," I chide. "You only have to do this for a few more days."

"I know!" She responds excitedly, blowing her hair out of her face, "It was starting to feel like I'd never get Amplified."

"You're telling me! I've been counting down the days ever since my brother got his."

"Speaking of your brother," Alia adds mischievously, "I saw him the other day. He looks delicious."

"Please don't ever refer to my brother that way again."

"What? He's filled out very nicely. You can't blame me for recognizing a fantastic male specimen when I see one."

"Okay, you have got to stop that."

"Or what? You'll pull a Miles Paxton?"

I chuckle dutifully at her comment, but the memory still feels a little too raw to joke about. Even though it's been three years since my friend Miles broke into the nutrition factory and disappeared, I still have nightmares about him. Nobody knew how he managed to get past the guards, but I had a fairly good idea. We used to practice the fighting techniques we saw in the films at school, which was forbidden, but we would find places where there were no cameras and fight with imaginary people, with bushes, or with each other. We got pretty good. He would tell me how he used to spy on the night guards at the factories and the control tower. He said that they were usually slow and drowsy from being up all night, especially when they would forget to command themselves to stay awake.

He would talk about stealing supplies and running away all the time, but I couldn't understand why he would want to give up the opportunity to be Amplified, so I never took him seriously. The night Miles went missing, an air barge hovered over our compound for hours, bright lights scouring every house and soldiers seeming to rain down from the sky in search of him. It wouldn't have been such a big deal except that he stole a whole crate of capsules, which no one had ever managed to do before.

The next morning, some Restrainers came into our school. They looked so intimidating in their shiny, official uniforms. I was fascinated by the Restrainers; people who work directly under Governor Plenaris and have enhanced Amplification to more effectively protect our Community. They told us we would be rewarded if we could tell them anything that might lead to Miles' whereabouts. I was tempted say something. I was worried about Miles and what would happen to him, but mostly I was mad that he left me behind. I felt betrayed. In the end though, Miles had never told me where he planned to go, so I couldn't give them any useful information anyway.

After two weeks of unsuccessful searching, The Restrainers sent a report back to Governor Plenaris saying that Miles had likely crossed out of the Community's transmitter range and perished in the open desert. Their assumption frightened me, but somehow I knew Miles was smarter than to just run off and collapse in the desert. I think other people assumed he wasn't stupid enough to wander off and die either, not someone who had gotten past a dozen Amplified guards and stolen a bunch of capsules. So he became a legend. Anything or anyone that goes missing for any amount of time is referred to as a "Miles Paxton." It's become a dangerous, albeit, severely overused expression. I guess some people think it's cool to mention him. For me, it just reopens the wound.

"This is so tedious!" Alia complains, bringing me back to the present. "Don't they have machines for this?"

"No," I say, clearing my throat, "with small crops like these, the machines can't differentiate between the weeds and the vegetables." Alia gives me a bored look. "That's why they need our nimble fingers," I add lamely, trying to sound more interesting.

"Mari, You know too much about useless things."

"Maybe," I respond. "But it's relevant to us right now, so it's not completely useless."

"Ok, whatever," Alia replies nonchalantly. She gestures to the crops we're weeding around. "Speaking of useless information, do you know what these taste like?"

I look down at the long, green vegetables. Beans, I think they're called.

"No. Why would I know that?"

Alia shrugs. "I don't know. You just seem like someone who'd be curious enough to try them."

I shake my head. "Not *that* curious."

Nobody eats the crops. When they're harvested, they go directly to the nutrition factory to be processed and encapsulated. Years ago, people used to eat the crops, some more than others. But then they started threatening to refuse or remove Amplification for eating them, and people promptly stopped. Nobody really does anything out of line anymore. They're too afraid of losing Amplification.

I look up and see my mother coming toward us, walking confidently down the rows of crops she's worked in for most of the last 16 years. My father used to work here too, before The 12-Hours Virus killed him and hundreds of others. That was a terrible time. The virus seemingly came from nowhere and was gone within a week, but once contracted, the victim only survived for about 12 hours, which is what gave the virus its name. Most of the Amplified were able to manipulate their bodies back to health, but those not Amplified simply weren't able to get medical help in time. My father was strong until the very end, not collapsing and weeping as many were doing. It was hard on my family, but my mother was calm and peaceful through it all. That was five years ago.

"Hello girls!" My mother calls cheerfully. "Are you enjoying this nice, warm weather?"

Warm is an understatement. We've been in the blistering sun for several hours now and I can feel sweat trickling down my back.

"Hello Felicia," Alia exclaims sweetly. I've always found it weird that she calls my mother by her first name. "It must be nice to have *Adrian* home again."
The way she says Adrian's name makes me nauseous and I stare at her, willing her not to say anything inappropriate about my brother again.

"It's been wonderful, although a bit of an adjustment," my mom confesses, furrowing her brow.

It *has* been an adjustment. We've loved hearing about all of Adrian's adventures and watching him show us all the things he can do, but I think he's stressing my mother out with his late nights and close calls with the Restrainers. He's probably just been restless with all this free time. In the next week or so he'll receive his work rotation and probably move to the city.

"Anyway," my mom continues, "I'm supposed to tell you two that you're off early today because you need to pick up your training uniforms in the city."

"Really?" Alia shrieks, jumping up from her knees, "That's the best news ever!"

She looks so elated, I don't have the heart to tell her she has a worm in her hair.

Chapter 4

"Adrian? Can I come in?" It feels odd to be knocking on the door to his room when I always used to walk right in, but now we're both older and I feel like I should respect his privacy. I hear Adrian mumble an assent so I crack open the door and see him lying on his bed, staring at the ceiling.

"Can I talk to you for a minute?" I ask, still wondering why I feel like I'm inconveniencing him. He props himself up on one elbow.

"Sure, what's up?"

I cross the room and sit on the only other piece of furniture besides the bed; a beautiful hand-carved wooden chair my dad made a few months before he died. I clear my throat and try to figure out if I actually want answers or just reassurance.

"I'm reporting for Training tomorrow, and I just feel..."

"Nervous?" Adrian offers. "That's pretty normal."

"No, I'm not nervous," I say slowly, running my seared finger along the pattern etched into the chair. "Well, I *am* nervous, but mostly I'm just worried about ... losing myself."

"What do you mean?"

"I don't know. It just seems like most people are different after they're Amplified, like they abandon everything that makes them unique." I bite my lip as I realize that lately I've accused Adrian of this very thing, but he seems unaffected, so I continue. "I mean, I think

Amplification is incredible, and I've been waiting for this for years, but I don't want to have to trade morals and memories for skills and abilities. If I could just-"

Suddenly Adrian lets out a loud laugh. Confused, I look at him more closely, and see the small Adhesive applied to his temple. I should have recognized his glazed eyes and the way he was looking at a point just above my head.

"You're watching a movie?" I exclaim, jumping out of the chair.

"Sorry sis!" He admits sheepishly. "But I was listening, I promise!"

"Really? What was I just saying?"

"That you're nervous about Training."

"I can't believe you."

"Hey, I wish I could stop it, but you know how it is with these Adhesives - once you stick them on, you just have to wait until they finish."

"I know," I retort coldly, turning to leave.

"Mari, just come back in an hour and then I can answer all your questions."

I walk out of the room and close the door behind me.

"You already did," I murmur.

————-

I've never particularly enjoyed looking at myself in the mirror, unlike Alia, who once told me she'll look for any excuse to see her reflection. But I want a good picture of what the other trainees will see tomorrow, so I put on my pale green Training uniform and force my eyes up to study my features. I have my mother's caramel skin and my father's auburn hair, but the look of defiance staring out from my large brown eyes is all my own. I look over the unbalanced portions of my body; my legs are too long and my torso too short, so the bottoms of my pants fall conspicuously above my ankles. Hopefully no one will notice if I let down the hem.

A big-eyed, angry-looking, gangly girl, that's what they'll see, I think. Shrugging my shoulders, I turn away from the mirror and gasp as I see my mother standing in the doorway.

"Sorry, honey, I didn't mean to startle you," she apologizes. "I just wanted to make sure everything is all right. You seem a little anxious."

I let out my breath. I have been a bit on edge today.

"I guess I'm still trying to process everything," I admit. "I'm ready to go to Training, but I wish I knew exactly what to expect."

"Sometimes the only way to know things is to experience them for yourself," she replies.

I frown. It's a simple statement, but I feel like she means something else. I change the subject and ask her the question I've probably asked a thousand times before.

"Mom, why did you never get Amplified?"

She smiles. "I have my reasons." Her expression is light, but her eyes are oddly lucid and intense. She's given a variation of this answer every time I've asked. Maybe one day she'll explain those reasons.

"It just doesn't seem right," I press. "How does it comply with the Equality Movement if some people are Amplified and some aren't?"

"We're equal in our desires," she responds.

————

I can't sleep. I keep looking out my small window, willing the sun to rise. How could anyone actually sleep the night before they get Amplified? I get out of bed and tip toe to the cabinet in the front room. Maybe a nutrition capsule will help ease my nausea. On my way back to bed, I hear muffled sounds coming from Adrian's room. I notice his door is cracked open so I quietly walk over and peek in. After a few seconds I realize that he's talking in his sleep. I move closer to the door, straining to catch his words.

"Adrian, do one thousand push-ups," he mumbles. I can imagine he has commanded himself to do that often in order to attain his current physique. He shifts in bed and mutters something else.

"Adrian, run faster!"

His breath quickens and he groans a little. I guess his words are coinciding with his dreams. I remember learning that in the early days of Amplification, people would often access their Amplifier accidentally by talking in their sleep, so it was modified to shut off when someone was unconscious. I'm grateful that modification was made, otherwise Adrian would likely wake everyone up with his compulsory exercising.

"Adrian, attack the Dissenters!" He whispers. I have to keep myself from laughing. It really isn't funny, him revisiting combat in his sleep, but the way he says it sounds like the self-important tone of a toddler pretending to wage war against an army of unsuspecting bushes. I watch him flinch a few times, then his breathing slows and his body appears to relax. I'm about to return to my room when I hear him speak again.

"Adrian, kill him."

My breath catches in my throat. I turn and quickly walk away, willing myself to forget the words my brother uttered so calmly in his subconscious.

Chapter 5

For the first time today, I feel the exhaustion setting in. It seems like an eternity since I said goodbye to my mother and brothers this morning, my sadness from leaving them overshadowed by the excitement of what was to come. "You'll s-send us messages, w-won't you Mari?" Daniel had asked pleadingly, probably recalling Adrian's lack of correspondence while he was in the Service. I had promised to send him an Adhesive message twice a month. Hopefully I'll have enough free time during Training to deliver on that promise.

The ride into the city on the Mall-cruiser with Alia and Joby was uneventful, I think we were all too agitated to sustain any real conversation. I heard the air barge before I saw it — hovering high above the landing field, it's dozens of long cables hanging down like tentacles. I was surprised when the Restrainers explained how to board the air barge; setting one foot in a loop at the end of a cable and holding on while the cables retracted into the barge. It seemed a little crazy, almost like some kind of initiation to make sure we really wanted to be Amplified. I was a little hesitant, but not as much as some others. A boy I remember from my class got hysterical and refused to board. It was pretty embarrassing for all of us, ashamed that anyone our age would act like that. I felt bad for him, but not too much. He was one of the boys who used to terrorize me for being the child of a *clam*.

The ascent up to the barge was absolutely exhilarating. Being hauled 500 feet into the air with only a cord to hold on to really has a way of heightening your senses. I could see our Community sprawling out below me, for the first time able to see its spider shape for myself instead of just in an image or film. I had glanced around at all the other trainees dangling in mid air as the cables slowly clicked back into the barge, inching us upward in unison. I started to sway a little bit to see what would happen, but when I bumped into Alia next to me, her severe stare was enough to make me stop. When we reached the edge of the barge, several Restrainers reached over and helped us onto the deck.

And now, we wait. I lean forward to look down the long row of trainees, arranged in alphabetical order, all of us clad in our pale green uniforms. We stand silently at attention as we watch new trainees emerge over the sides of the air barge, about 20 or so from each compound. They used to have to do Training separately for each compound, but over the last few decades, less and less people have been having children, so it's just been more efficient to combine all the trainees from the Community into one Training group.

I gaze out across the expanse of the barge. It seems almost empty with only us trainees and a handful of Restrainers lining a small corner of the massive structure. It's a bit eerie, actually, like a floating ghost town. We're completely exposed to the open sky, standing just a couple feet away from the precarious edges. I keep glancing at the squat buildings scattered across the gray surface, half-expecting something or someone to jump out at us. Joby, who is several feet down from me, is shuffling his feet over one of the many uniform fissures in the floor. He never was any good at holding still. Across from me, I see Alia eyeing a tall blonde boy next to her.

Scanning the faces of my fellow trainees, I see various expressions of fear, anxiety, boredom, and curiosity. Some are staring with wide eyes, taking everything in, and others are trying to adjust their ears to this new altitude or fight off fatigue. I guess I'm not the only one who had a restless night. I meet the eyes of a conspicuously chubby boy who looks like he's trying very hard to make himself look smaller. It's unusual for anyone to be overweight, but I noticed a few of the trainees from his compound were pretty large. Maybe they have different kinds of nutrition capsules. I smile at him and his eyes light up. He seems nice.

Suddenly, the relatively quiet atmosphere goes silent. A tall woman, apparently our head trainer, emerges from the building closest to us. She looks about 30, but it's hard to pin down ages in Amplified people, especially when they manipulate their aging processes. Her long, dark hair is pulled back, accenting her sharp green eyes and revealing the angles in her face. Her dark blue uniform fits tightly over her stunning body. Her expression is cold and unwelcoming, but it's difficult to look away from her — she commands attention.

She walks toward us briskly, her eyes scanning everyone but not looking at anyone directly. She nods at the Restrainers, who promptly vacate the barge by jumping over the side. I'd be alarmed, but I'm sure they have some kind of mechanism on their suits to help them reach the ground safely. Once the woman has reached the center of our formation, she narrows her eyes and speaks.

"Talina, deliver the orientation speech."

Her eyes lose their severity as her Amplifier takes over. Her voice, which a second ago was shrill and direct, becomes a lazy monotone as she recites stored information.

"The Amplification project was founded approximately two centuries ago in an effort to assist persons with paralysis, rehabilitation, and other illnesses."

I remember watching the film of the first Amplifier in school. No matter how many times I watched it, I never got sick of it. The man they tested was paralyzed from the neck down, and the Amplifier was a huge apparatus he wore around his head, long before they streamlined the technology down to a small implant behind the ear. When he commanded himself to stand up and walk, his body responded, and he looked so overwhelmed. Everyone in the room with him was cheering and crying.

I pull myself out of my memories and concentrate on listening to Talina as she drones on.

"Over time, those with Amplifiers became far more capable than ordinary humans, creating a large disparity in advantages and opportunities between the two groups. Therefore, the Equality Movement was instituted, allowing every qualified individual the choice to receive Amplification, conditional upon their agreement to 4 years of Service and 35 years in work rotations."

I cringe a little. Of course I always knew that these were the terms, but hearing the numbers formally makes my mouth go sour. That's almost 40 years of my life planned out for me! I suppose that's the price I'll have to pay in order to be ultimately capable.

"You have the right to request the removal of your Amplifier at any time, but be advised that once the implant has been extracted, you will not have another opportunity for Amplification."

I hear someone snicker. I can imagine what they're thinking. *Why would anyone choose to go back to being normal once they'd experienced being superior?*

"You are expected to comply with all Training regulations and procedures. If you are found in violation of any of the rules set forth by the Community or by your trainers, your Amplifier will be removed and you will be sent home. Furthermore, should you fail to conform to the standards of Amplification, your Amplifier will be removed, and you will be sent home. This Training will culminate in a final assessment. If you fail the assessment, your Amplifier will be removed, and you will be sent home. "

I stifle a yawn. It's hard to keep myself awake when I've heard all of this information hundreds of times before. At least I'm doing better than the boy on my left, who seems to keep swaying back and forth. I steal a sideways glance at him and notice that his face is completely pale. Just as I'm trying to decide if I should be worried about him, his eyes roll up into his head and he starts falling straight back toward the edge of the barge.

I should alert Talina. I should make a plan. I should ask for help. There's a million things I should do, but there's no time. This guy is about to go over the edge and nobody's doing anything. So I move.

Chapter 6

The boy is still unconscious and falling quickly as I dive at him and grab his arm. I manage to jerk his body sideways as we slam to the floor of the barge, but the momentum of his fall causes him to roll over the edge and he's taking me with him. I feel his hand grip my arm and hear frantic screaming coming from below the deck where he's dangling. He must have regained consciousness. I'm sliding, struggling to find something for my feet to grip, but the surface is too slick.

Why isn't anybody helping? I wonder, desperately trying to find a way to hold on. *Are they all just going to watch us fall thousands of feet to our death?* He's heavier than me, and with no hold, our fate seems inevitable. I'm almost halfway over when I see a small green button right underneath the ledge. I can just make out the words: "CABLE RELEASE." Hoping it means what I think it does, and with no other immediate option, I slam the button with my fist as we slip completely over the edge.

For a split-second it seems like I will die, falling head first into the silent, endless air. And then I glimpse the looped end of a cable emerging from a small compartment under the barge. I twist around and try to grasp it with my free hand, but it's beyond my reach. It's just as well, my grip wouldn't have been strong enough to hold both of us anyway. Looking back up at the cable, I concentrate all my effort on getting my foot in the loop and pray for a miracle.

My left foot catches, and I feel the cable give a little as it absorbs our weight. *That's lucky*, I think, *otherwise I probably would have broken my ankle.* But I don't have much time to bask in my answered prayer. I feel sharp pains in my wrist and look down to see the boy clawing hysterically up my arm.

"Help me! I'm slipping! I'm going to die!" He shrieks in between shallow breaths. He's holding my arm in a vice-like grip with both of his hands, and his beady eyes dart around wildly. I have a fleeting thought that maybe this kid wasn't worth saving, but it's overshadowed by a more pressing thought: *If this guy keeps climbing up my arm, he'll probably tear my head off.*

"Calm down!" I yell at him. I look around and notice all the other cables inching out around us, and I get an idea. "Listen, I'm going to swing you over to another cable. You'll be able to hold on better and it will be safer for both of us."

"What?" He squeals. "No! I can't do it! You're just trying to get rid of me!"

I decide not to expend my energy trying to talk sense into him. Instead, I put my other foot into the loop of the cable to secure my hold, and start swaying my upside-down body back and forth, despite loud and vicious protests from my obstinate cargo. We pick up speed, and are soon swinging within grasping range of some of the other cables.

"Just reach out on the next pass and grab hold of one of the loops, okay?" I relay hopefully. I'm not sure if it's all the blood rushing to my head or the actual state of things, but he looks like he's twitching. He makes a feeble attempt on the first pass, barely allowing his hand to leave my arm. On the next pass he flings one arm out violently and successfully grabs a cable, but still holds fast to my arm with his other hand.

His death grip on my arm pries me loose from my cable, and I flip down, smashing right into him. He releases me at the impact, and I have to scramble to grab onto his legs. I smell urine. *Of course,* I think. *Of course he wet himself.*

"Hey! Get off me!" He screams, shaking his legs viciously. My extreme dislike for this guy is growing by the minute. But I have to act fast, because if he insists on using all of his strength trying to get rid of me, he'll lose his grip on his cable and it'll be over for both of us.

I take a deep breath and once again start rocking my body back and forth, building up the momentum needed to get me close to the other cables. The kid is writhing and screaming with hysteria, but I do my best to ignore him. Just as I'm cresting and planning to jump on the next pass, the boy gives me a fierce kick in the face and I'm abruptly dislodged, floating backwards though the air.

For a moment, I experience a feeling of complete euphoria; pure, weightless, freedom. But in the next moment, the full gravity of my situation turns my elation into terror. I struggle to look behind me, trying to locate any cables nearby, but I can't see any. I get a sinking feeling (literally) that I've fallen too far below the cables to be able to reach anything.

Then I see something pass by my ear, and I grab at it instinctively. My hands burn as I grasp the cable, the grooves in the metal ripping through my fingers, but I don't let go. Finally, I slide to a stop just above the loop at the end. I use my last bit of energy to pull myself up and plant my feet in the loop to give my now raw fingers a rest.

Several cables away, the boy is yelling at me, but I can't hear what he's saying. I watch his flushed, swollen face with mild interest, wondering what profanities he might be screaming. His white-blonde hair is plastered to his face with sweat, and he looks like an angry baby. After a few minutes, the cables catch and start inching us back up toward the barge. I close my eyes and review the events of the last few minutes. I am so lucky I'm still alive.

————-

"There they are!"

I hear shouting and chatter as we near the deck of the barge. I look up to see everyone crowded at the edge, peeking over cautiously and pointing at us. A dozen hands reach out to help me over the side. Through the melee, Talina breaks through and looks me over, apparently checking me for injuries. She's saying something, but I can't make it out. I focus harder on the words, but they still don't make sense.

"When in combat, or in other emergency situations where exact cooperation is required, you will be subjected to an Authoritative Override..."

Finally, I understand. She's still giving the orientation lecture. The command she gave herself will stay in effect until its completion. Until then, she can't speak independently, but the anger in her eyes conveys exactly how she's feeling. Still speaking, she turns, motions to everyone to stay where they are, and disappears into the squat building from which she entered.

Before I can even collect myself, somebody crashes into my side, knocking me to the ground.

"What were you trying to do, kill me?" The blonde kid is on top of me, spraying me with spit as he shouts in my face. Thoroughly annoyed now, I shove the guy off of me and stand up.

"I saved your life, you idiot! You passed out!"

"Are you kidding? You attacked me!"

"To keep you from falling off the edge!"

I notice some of the others are eyeing me suspiciously. I'm defensive, but I suppose it might have looked like I attacked him if they hadn't seen the whole situation from the beginning.

Suddenly, everyone straightens. Talina has emerged from the building, looking stern.

"Marianna Quillen and Tristan Prewitt, come with me," she barks. "Everyone else will follow Justin to the dormitories."

41

At least now I have a name to put with the face I've come to hate. I should have known it'd be something lame like *Tristan*. I follow Talina into the building while the others file off after a stocky guy with long hair. I'm guessing he's the assistant trainer. We descend a narrow flight of stairs into a small, dark room. Two of the walls are covered in controls and screens. It smells acidic.

Talina turns to face us, her expression more perturbed than ever.

"Tell me what happened."

Tristan is the first to open his stupid mouth.

"I was just standing there, listening, when out of nowhere she attacks me and pushes me over the side!"

Talina raises her eyebrow at me. I sigh and offer my version of the story.

"I noticed he was losing consciousness and was starting to fall off the barge. So I grabbed him, but we both went over the edge anyway."

"Oh, please!" Tristan interjects. "No one risks their life to save a stranger!" I roll my eyes, but Talina is nodding in agreement.

"True, but the other alternative is that she risked her life to kill you, which also doesn't seem likely."

There are a million things I want to say, but I force myself to be silent. Somehow, I've become the irrational one in the room.

"Unfortunately," Talina continues, "I won't be able to make any conclusions until they send me a copy of the camera surveillance tomorrow morning. Until then, both of your Amplifications will be delayed."

"What?" Tristan exclaims. "This isn't fair! First I'm nearly killed and then I have to wait to be Amplified?"

Although I refuse to whine about it, I share Tristan's sentiments exactly.

Chapter 7

I feel out of place. The recreation lounge is full of laughing, hopeful, excited teenagers, trying out their newly Amplified skills in the trampoline rooms and on the aerial obstacle course. Tonight is supposed to be a relaxing, social mixer before Training officially starts tomorrow, but I've never felt more on edge. Mostly everyone is avoiding me, even Alia abandoned me to talk to the blonde boy she was standing next to earlier today. Although, she did ask me several times if I'd mind before she did. I watch her flirting with him across the room and realize I can't blame her, she always follows her heart, and he is pretty good looking.

Tristan doesn't seem to be here, which is a relief. He's probably in his room moping. Or plotting revenge. I search the lounge to find something to distract me from the memory of what happened earlier, but it's difficult when everything reminds me that I'm the only one in here that's not Amplified.

"It's been quite the day, hasn't it?"

I jump at the sound of Joby's voice. Sometimes he can be so quiet. I didn't hear him come up behind me.

"Yeah," I respond bitterly, "it's definitely exceeded all my expectations."

"I wouldn't worry about it," Joby says as he sits down next to me. "I bet it'll make a really good story later on."

I appreciate his effort, and he's probably right, but somehow I just can't be so confident about it right now. I look over at Joby, glad to finally have some company. His red, curly hair is so long, it falls over his half-closed eyes, but he doesn't make any effort to brush it out of the way. Instead he taps his pale fingers restlessly on the side of the chair. That's the thing about Joby, he's always moving, but never in a way that accomplishes anything.

"So, how was it?" I ask.

"How was what?"

"Getting Amplified this afternoon?"

"It hurt a little, but the pain went away after a couple hours."

I know Joby is downplaying it for my benefit, but I really am curious.

"But how does if *feel* to be Amplified?" I probe. "Did you do anything cool?"

"Well..."

"Come on, just tell me!"

Joby smiles slyly.

"Ok," he concedes excitedly, "the first thing I did after I got my Amplifier was tell myself to go to sleep."

I burst out laughing. He looks at me defensively, but I can't help it.

"Joby, you had the opportunity to try almost anything and you choose to make yourself fall asleep?"

He looks down at his feet, clearly hurt. I feel guilty now. This is no way to treat the one person who's being nice to me tonight.

"I'm sorry I laughed," I murmur apologetically. "But of all things, why did you choose *that*?"

45

"I've always had a really hard time falling asleep," Joby confesses. "Sometimes I'll lay awake in bed for four or five hours before I doze off. Sometimes I'll stay awake the whole night. So being able to tell myself to sleep and having it happen immediately was miraculous for me."

Now I feel even more guilty. Not only did I laugh at something that has been a huge struggle for him, I've also never asked him why he is so tired all the time. I just figured he was lazy. Some friend I am.

"That's really incredible, Joby," I admit. "I'm glad you'll be able to sleep better."

"I guess it was kinda lame," Joby says, trying to lighten the mood. "I didn't wake up until someone tripped over me in the dorm room."

"Wait, you fell asleep on the floor?"

"Yeah, I didn't want to wait to find my bed."

This time Joby laughs along with me. Maybe I wasn't completely wrong about him being lazy.

"Have you tried that yet?" I ask him, pointing to the aerial course.

"No, there were too many people on it," Joby hedges.

"Maybe before," I observe, "but now there's hardly anyone. You should try it."

Joby gulps.

"Hey, you can do anything, remember?" I tease, tapping behind his ear where the Amplifier is embedded. He flinches, the skin is probably still a little raw, but then he resolutely stands and walks to the platform at the beginning of the obstacle course.

He straps himself into the bungee harness, then walks a few steps back, causing the bungee line to tighten. His eyes scan the course and he says something to himself, probably making a command through his Amplifier. He pushes the launch button. The platform pulls him back several feet, and then he is abruptly launched into the air, sailing toward the first obstacle, which is a grouping of several large hoops suspended from the high ceiling.

I hold my breath as he maneuvers expertly through the hoops. It really is odd to see Joby, who rarely moves more than is absolutely necessary, display such amazing athleticism. He reaches the small platform that precedes the tightrope. Well, "tightrope" is a loose term for this contraption; a taut line that vibrates, jerks, and loosens at random. He pauses to give himself a command, then steps forward.

Almost instantly the rope jolts to the side and he is thrown off, but he catches the rope with one hand and swings himself back to stand upright on the line. He flings his arms wildly back and forth for a few moments, trying to find his balance, then sets his face and begins to run across the rope. Every step is sure and nimble, even when the rope loosens so dramatically that he is momentarily running through the air. He picks up speed to the end of the line and falls right into the Plunge, an aptly named portion of the course that drops you 80 feet into a hole in the floor. Joby disappears into the hole, and I wonder how much farther the drop continues. I can't imagine the air barge is very deep, but I suppose I have yet to learn all the mysteries of this structure.

Just as I start to worry, I hear the turbines gear up, and a second later, Joby comes shooting out of the floor. He jerks around in the air, trying to get himself oriented. The turbines shut off, and he starts to fall back down again, going into the hole for the second time. Some barricades prevent anyone from standing too close to the course, but I walk over and stand right next to them. I crane my neck, trying to peer down into the hole, but all I can see is blackness.

The next moment I'm knocked backwards by the force of the turbines turning on. I fall to the floor as Joby launches into view, much more composed in the air this time. He rolls forward to escape the air stream and grabs the first of several metal bars, placed at varying heights and unevenly spaced. I watch Joby performing intricate acrobatics to get from one bar to the next. I'm in awe.

"I bet everything looks impressive to someone who's not Amplified."

I look behind me and see the boy Alia was flirting with earlier. His otherwise handsome face is ruined by an ugly sneer. I look around and see that everyone in the room is staring at me. I quickly get to my feet.

"Yes, it is impressive," I retort. "Seeing a normal person do extraordinary things through an Amplifier is incredible."

"Well, I guess we need to have someone around to marvel at the rest of us, *clam*."

I hear a few snickers coming from behind him. I move in a little closer.

"Well, oh mighty, Amplified one," I whisper sarcastically, "don't expect me to come after *you* when you fall off the barge."

His face goes slack. I turn around and walk quickly out of the lounge.

Just what I need, I think. *More people that hate me.*

I've almost made it to the hall that leads to my dorm when I hear Joby call out behind me.

"Mari, are you all right?"

I exhale slowly. There are so many things I want to say, but it wouldn't be fair to take my frustrations out on Joby, who seems like my only friend right now.

"I'm fine," I respond evenly without turning around. I remember that I didn't see Joby finish the course, and I note with some disgust at myself that I don't care.

"Well," Joby adds uncertainly, "everything is going to work out."

It seems like such a trite thing to say, but I know Joby means it, so I turn to him and smile.

"Thanks, Joby. See you tomorrow."

But as I lay in bed in my empty dorm, I can't help but feel that everything is *not* going to work out. Even if they do allow me to be Amplified, it seems like I'm entering a world with entirely different rules, procedures, and moral codes. A world where it's a crime to risk your life to save someone else.

Chapter 8

When Talina said, "early in the morning," she wasn't lying.

It seemed like I had just drifted off to sleep when a few seconds later, someone was shaking me awake, telling me it was time for my review. I'm pretty groggy from two nights of bad sleep, but the cold morning air jerks me from my sluggishness as I wait outside the building we met in with Talina yesterday. Tristan stands across from me, looking sour. He seems to be focusing on a small spot by his feet.

Finally, the doors open and Talina steps out, looking nearly immaculate despite the heavy circles under her eyes. She gestures for us to follow her into the building. We descend to the same room, and everything looks identical to the way it was yesterday except for one thing: Governor Plenaris.

The sight of our Governor used to make me excited; I would imagine ways to show my loyalty, to make him proud. But now, seeing him standing in front of me in the flesh, with his slicked back hair and prominent nose, all I feel is an intense fear. Was our incident really so extraordinary that it warrants a visit from the Community's highest official? The man who oversees all Amplification?

"Tristan, Marianna, take a seat," Talina instructs. We sit down on chairs that are so uncomfortable, it seems intentional. Talina sits on a table across the room, but the Governor remains standing.

"Of course you'll recognize Governor Plenaris," she adds coolly. "Because this circumstance is so extraneous, he's come to review the situation." The Governor's detached expression does not change as he gives a slight nod in our direction. Talina continues. "We have already gone over yesterday's surveillance, but we'd like to watch it again with the two of you present."

Talina presses a few buttons on the control panel next to her, and suddenly my face is on every screen in the room. I shrink back in my chair. It's a little unnerving to be staring back at myself from every angle. The surveillance pans out to reveal Tristan, pale and dazed, intermittently swaying next to me. We watch his eyes roll back and his body stiffen as he starts to topple over the edge. In the footage, my eyes widen and I quickly glance around before propelling myself toward him.

The surveillance clearly illustrates a rescue attempt, and Tristan probably realizes this because I notice he reddens and sinks in his chair. I try not to show too much relief. I can feel Talina and the Governor watching me closely for my reaction, so I try to assume an appropriately concerned expression as the rest of the footage is replayed. When it shows us being pulled back onto the barge, Talina hits a button and the screens go blank.

"Well, Mr. Prewitt," Talina says, looking at Tristan, "it seems the altitude affected you. Luckily, that is something that can be easily fixed with Amplification. Please report to the Implantation Building immediately.

Miss Quillen, please remain here, we'd like to speak with you a moment."

Here we go, I think, wondering how I'm going to explain to my mother that I got sent home for helping someone. Tristan stands sheepishly, but smirks at me before he leaves. Once he's gone, Talina turns to me.

"We're interested, *Marianna*," she says my name sharply, like she's slapping me in the face with her voice, "in how you knew to react so quickly."

How I knew *to react?* Several possible answers run through my mind. Practicing fighting moves with Miles, the games my parents would have us play, building speed and strength from running all the time ... but I don't feel comfortable giving them any of those explanations, so I play dumb instead.

"I don't know," I answer.

"So you didn't receive any special training or education prior to coming here?"

"No. Ma'am," I add, and regret it almost instantly. *Who says ma'am?* But Talina seems unfazed.

"Did you have any advantage in going after Tristan? Did you know him?"

"I'd never seen him before yesterday."

"Then why did you go to extreme measures to save him?"

"I don't know," I repeat, "it just seemed like the right thing to do."

Talina sighs and looks at Governor Plenaris. He nods and turns to address me.

"As you know, we look down on anyone striving to set themselves apart through unnecessary heroics, as set forth in the guidelines of the Equality Movement," he states. His voice is a little more shrill than I'm used to. They must alter it for the holograms.

"We've not seen this kind of behavior from a non-Amplified individual for a long time, and we are taking precautions, as this type of behavior is a threat to the Amplification system."

Well, that explains why no one else moved an inch yesterday. I know I'm different, but I didn't think my actions would be viewed as 'unnecessary heroics.' Someone was about to fall to their death, so I acted.

"With all due respect, sir," I begin shakily, "I don't understand why these circumstances should keep me from becoming Amplified."

"You will be Amplified, Marianna," he assures, "but you will be heavily monitored. Even though you are a risk, you can be a strong addition to the Community, granted that you align to certain standards of conformity."

"Oh, okay," I respond as I nod my head slowly, uncertain how to react. I'll get my Amplifier, which is good, but I wish everyone would stop treating me like I have some kind of disease. The Governor turns quickly to Talina, his crisp black suit rustling with the sudden movement.

"I expect a weekly report on Miss Quillen's progress and activities," he asserts. "I will return in several weeks to personally assess her situation."

"Noted," Talina answers grimly.

Governor Plenaris glances at each of us, his bright eyes flashing as he looks at me, then turns and swiftly exits the room. When we hear the door shut at the top of the stairs, Talina exhales, apparently in relief. She faces me and smiles. It's the first time I've seen her look friendly.

"Okay, then," she announces, "let's get you Amplified."

————-

The administrator has a unibrow. I try not to stare at it as she prepares my Amplifier, but it takes a great deal of effort. I attempt to distract myself with something else, but there aren't many things of interest in the brightly lit, sterile operating room. Sitting in the lone chair, I scan the blank white walls, the drab ceiling, and the spotless tiled floor. The space is immaculate. The administrator, I think she said her name was Lisa, works over a small cart, assembling instruments and entering data into a Transcriber.

I'm still a little overwhelmed at all the events that have transpired in the last two days. I'm thrilled to finally be getting Amplified, but I'm wary about the heavy monitoring I'll be under and the general disapproval I received from Governor Plenaris. There was a time that I would have been ecstatic to have seen him face to face, much less spoken with him, but now, thinking about our meeting just leaves me with a stale taste in my mouth.

Lisa, now finished with her preparations, approaches me with a large needle.

"I'm going to inject a numbing agent behind your ear."

Now I'm grateful for her unibrow - I have something to focus on while the needle goes into my skin. Soon I notice all the feeling leaving the area she injected, but I know exactly what she's doing thanks to her verbalized commands. She makes a small incision and cuts away some tissue. She then inserts the Amplifier, which is a flat, tiny square with dozens of almost invisible wires that automatically attach themselves to my nerves and glands. I get goosebumps as I imagine the minuscule tentacles wrapping around parts of my nervous system, taking a relentless hold that won't be interrupted unless the Amplifier is deactivated or broken.

Finally, she seals up the incision, disposes of her instruments, and retrieves the Transcriber.

"Full name?" She asks.

"Marianna Quillen."

"And the name you will use to direct your Amplifier?"

"Mari."

"Good." She enters the information into the device. "Please give yourself a command to activate your Amplifier."

I hesitate. I know what I want to do as my first act of Amplification - it's something I decided on years ago. But after meeting with the Governor, I wonder if it would be considered too much. I don't want to set myself apart more than I already have. Lisa is looking at me expectantly. *Would she care?* I wonder. Certainly this woman with a unibrow has seen far more elaborate stunts than the one I plan to do. I decide to go for it. I stand and walk a few paces away from the chair.

"Mari, do a double back flip."

My body comes to life. I feel myself go into a deep squat, and just as I'm wondering if the ceilings are high enough, my legs spring upward and my back arches. My knees snap up to my chest and my neck forces my head down, even though I'm straining to see the room as it spins around me. I catch a glimpse of Lisa once, twice, and then my feet hit the floor and my body straightens.

My shins are burning from the hard landing, but adrenaline pulses through me. I look up at Lisa with a goofy, openmouthed smile, but she is expressionless. She enters something into her Transcriber.

"You may go," she states indifferently. "I believe your Training has already started in building 119."

I nod and turn to leave. Clearly, mine wasn't the most outrageous move she's seen, which is a relief. At least I know this probably won't raise any flags in my report. But I can't help feeling a little bit disappointed that I didn't stand out. Maybe their accusation of "unnecessary heroics" wasn't that far off the mark.

Chapter 9

"What was he like? Did you talk to him? Is his hair really that stiff in person?"

I've made the mistake of divulging the details of my meeting this morning to Alia, and now she's excitedly bombarding me with questions. We're all on our way to the nutrition hall for a welcome break after listening to Talina's lectures for the past 4 hours. I now know more about the history and technology of Amplification than I could have ever imagined.

"I'll tell you when we get into the hall," I whisper to Alia. I'm secretly hoping she'll forget about it by the time we get there, but it's not likely. Alia is pretty tenacious when it comes to finding out juicy information.

The nutrition hall looks like any other building on the barge, just bigger. And it smells like chemicals. Large capsule dispensers line the far wall, and roughly 20 tables are scattered around the room, but there are no chairs. I don't mind, though. I've been sitting long enough today.

We line up behind all the other trainees at the dispensers. As we move slowly forward, I wonder why it's taking so long. Then I realize that every dispenser holds a different type of capsule. Close enough to read the labels now, I can only really understand about half of them. I pick up a small bowl and take one capsule from each dispenser: Regular, Protein, Energy, Stamina, Pacify, Satisfy, Pleasure, and Digest.

Alia and I find an empty table farthest from the dispensers. We set down our bowls, almost identical in their contents, and Alia looks at me expectantly.

"What?"

"Governor Plenaris?" Alia prompts.

"Oh, yeah," I sigh. While I was considering all the different capsules, I had momentarily forgotten about the unpleasantness of my review. But Alia is staring at me in anticipation, so I reluctantly recount my morning.

"I guess what happened was pretty unusual, and that's why the Governor had to be called in."

"What was he wearing?" Alia interjects.

"Um ... a nice black suit..."

"What about his shoes?"

"Some kind of boots, I think ... they had heels..."

"Heels?"

"Well, not heels, really. But they were raised." Suddenly, a voice from behind interrupts our conversation.

"Mind if we join you?"

We turn around to see Joby and the overweight boy I had noticed during orientation yesterday approaching our table.

"Not at all!" I exclaim, grateful for a reprieve from Alia's interrogation of the Governor's wardrobe. She glares at me, but I pretend not to notice.

"This is Liam," Joby announces, gesturing to the rotund boy as they slide their bowls across the table. I notice Liam's bowl is overflowing with pink Pleasure capsules.

"Have you tried these?" Liam asks, nodding at his bowl. He must have noticed me looking at them.

"No, not yet," I respond a little sheepishly, even though there was no accusation in his voice.

"They're addictive," he admits. "In our compound, they give these as rewards for good behavior."

"Then you must have been a very good boy," Alia hints rudely, looking pointedly at his large stomach. I want to kick her leg under the table, but she's too far away. Liam, however, doesn't seem to take any offense.

"I was a perfect boy," he jokes, patting his protruding belly and winking. Alia bursts into laughter and we all join in. I'm glad that some people here aren't as sensitive as Tristan.

"Did you have all these different capsules in your compound?" I ask Liam.

"All except for the Digest ones," he answers. "Those are only available to the Amplified."

"Oh. What do they do?"

"They do what they're named to do; speed up your digestion."

"You mean — " I start, but I can't quite find the words to finish.

"They make sure everything that goes in the top comes out the bottom within an hour," Liam explains impishly.

"Gross," Alia blurts out, but I can see her eyeing her Digest capsule with interest. I set mine aside to try later, I don't want to be running to the bathroom in the middle of Talina's lectures. I turn to my bowl of colorful capsules as the others carry on about Digestion.

I eat the Regular capsule first, and confirm my suspicion that these are the ones I've eaten my whole life. Next I try the Satisfy, and immediately I feel full and content, like I'm back at home listening to my mother's stories. The Protein capsule is salty and chalky, I can't imagine how Adrian could have enjoyed them, and the Pacify makes me feel calm and a little bit sleepy. Energy and Stamina taste and feel about the same, except that Energy is a little more intense. I'm glad I ate those after Pacify. Finally, I pop the Pleasure capsule in my mouth and am immediately overcome with a sickly sweet flavor. I don't know how anyone could find these addictive.

"You okay, Mari?" I glance up from my empty bowl and see Joby looking at me with a puzzled expression. My dislike for the Pleasure capsule must show on my face.

"That's the worst thing I've ever tasted," I say, nearly gagging on my still-sweet tongue. "Is there any Hydration in here?"

Liam laughs and points to the corner opposite the capsule dispensers. As I start walking toward the Hydration capsules, Liam calls out:

"Don't worry, Mari! They require a very sophisticated palate!"

————-

"Because your orientation was cut short due to circumstances beyond our control, I'm going to review some items that you may have missed," Talina informs us as she pulls a file up on the screens. I notice that several people steal a glance at me, knowing in part I'm the reason we have to review this boring information, but at least not all of them are looking at me with animosity this time.

There's a lazy, complacent feeling prevailing now that we've all filled ourselves with nutrition. I feel air coming from somewhere, even though I can't locate any windows or vents in the large, enclosed lecture room. It looks a lot like the operation room in the Implantation Building, gray and clean, but with higher ceilings. There are just enough chairs for all the trainees, probably another tactic to keep everyone feeling equal. I watch Talina organizing some files on the screen. It really must be a task keeping the attention of about 150 teenagers who have just been given immense abilities.

"First," Talina says loudly, causing more than a few drowsy heads to jerk upwards, "when commanding your Amplifier, you must start with your name. This is to protect yourself and others from sarcastic or flippant comments." I smile as I imagine people being forced to act on their offhand remarks. There would likely be far too much jumping off cliffs or eating worms.

"Second," Talina continues, "as some of you may have learned last night, you cannot use your Amplifier to enhance your anatomy." Talina looks pointedly at a group of boys in front of her who are ducking their heads and reddening. I hear a few snickers from around the room, but personally, I'm a little disappointed. *Oh well*, I think, *I guess I'll always be flat-chested.*

"Third," Talina snaps, regaining everyone's attention, "when you command yourself, you must be specific. You can't merely tell yourself to exercise, fight, or win. You must specify which maneuvers, how many, and how long. You have to put forth at least a little effort, the Amplifier is not going to do everything for you. On that note, the Amplifier will only perform actions that you have previously experienced, seen, or heard. It cannot fabricate behavior that is not already stored in your memory, although it can piece together new sequences of stored information if you direct it to do so." Talina pauses and looks out at us, presumably to see if anyone has any questions. There are none. Even if I did have a question, the intimidating look on Talina's face would discourage me from asking it.

"Lastly, we will go over the situations that cause your Amplifiers to shut off." Talena turns and opens a file on the screen. "Number one: when you are asleep." An old video starts to play. "This is why."

The video shows a man sleeping in a sparse room with a large window. He tosses back and forth in his bed, muttering incomprehensible words. Suddenly he sits up, alert, though his eyes are glazed over. "Andrew," he yells, "collect the samples." He busies himself by looking in an imaginary microscope and picking out invisible items from his bed sheets. I hear a few stifled giggles across the room.

"Andrew, punch him in the stomach." The man stares at a point on the wall for a moment, then jumps out of his bed, rushes forward, and slams his fist in a low uppercut into the wall. Most of us are full out laughing now, watching as he struggles to get his fist out of the hole he just created in the wall. He frees his hand and stares at the wall blankly, then turns abruptly.

"Andrew, run to headquarters." He launches into a full sprint toward the window. Our laughter ceases as he smashes through the glass and trips over the low sill. We hear a sickening thump and the video goes blank.

"He fell four stories," Talina comments to the still silent room. Nobody asks what became of Andrew because nobody wants to know.

"Next," Talina plows on, "loss of voice will render your Amplifiers useless." A picture of a hysterical-looking woman with a large metal contraption wrapped around her mouth appears on the screen.

"This is a muzzle," Talina explains. "They are very heavy, nearly impossible to remove, and extremely effective. They are also the best resource the Dissenters currently have against us."

Her last comment confuses me. I can't imagine the Dissenters being in possession of such sleek and useful equipment. At least not the idiotic, dopey-looking people I've been taught were Dissenters, the ones who oppose Amplification because they aren't fit to be Amplified. Maybe they've become more sophisticated over the last few years. Or maybe the Community has been showing us false images to dumb down our perceptions of the real threat. The more I learn about our system, the more the latter seems likely.

A boy in the back of the room asks a question.

"How do you remove the muzzle?"

"With an Override, which we will talk about more extensively in a few minutes," Talina responds. "The last thing that will shut down your Amplifier is Intoxication. I've asked Jaren to help me demonstrate this principle. Jaren?"

I watch the tall, rude, blonde guy that Alia's been fawning over stand and walk to the front. He gives a quick wink to Alia, and I feel her squirm with delight next to me. My stomach churns.

"Please take this Intoxication capsule," Talina says simply, handing the multicolored pill to Jaren. He hardly looks at it before popping it in his mouth. After a few seconds his eyes widen and he smiles a little.

"What is this?" He asks with obvious interest.

"That is unimportant," Talina snaps. "Now give yourself a command."

"Okay," Jaren answers cockily. He cracks his neck and assumes a wide stance. "Jaren, do a 5-second hand stand." Nothing happens. He looks sideways at Talina, who shrugs. He tries again, this time speaking a little more clearly.

"Jaren, do a 5-second handstand."

Again, nothing happens. Frustrated, he tries a different command.

"Jaren, jump up and touch the ceiling." This time he jumps with his arms outstretched, but his reach falls a few feet short of the ceiling. Clearly, he attempted the maneuver on his own. He stares angrily at Talina.

"This is ridiculous!" He spits out. "I don't even feel intoxicated at all!"

"That is the point," Talina counters. "It doesn't matter if you've had one or one hundred, once the Amplifier registers that you have Intoxication in your system, it will not perform. This is also why Intoxication is strictly forbidden during Training." Jaren pouts and jams his fists in his pockets.

"How long will this last?" He grumbles.

"About four hours, when the toxins are completely flushed from your system." Jaren opens his mouth to complain, but Talina cuts him off. "You can speed up the process with one of these," she adds, handing him a Digest capsule. "Thank you for your help."

Jaren takes the capsule begrudgingly and slumps back to his seat.

"Looks like your boyfriend doesn't do too well with performance issues," I whisper to Alia.

"Shut up, Mari!" She hisses back, but I can see she's fighting back a smile.

"Finally, we will discuss the Override," Talina announces, turning back to the screen. "Generally, your Amplifiers will only be overridden during battle, although there are other special circumstances where the Override might be appropriate, such as removing a muzzle." Now the screen shows a video of thousands of soldiers in a forested area. It soon becomes clear that they are participating in some kind of simulated battle, but it's hard to tell exactly what is going on in all of the chaos. Some soldiers are engaged in hand to hand combat, others are using stunt weapons, while still others are running in every direction or scaling trees.

"The leaders of the Community decided that it would be far less stressful in battle if all soldiers were directed by a third party, thus saving huge amounts of time that otherwise would have been spent learning and practicing formations, tactics, and strategies," Talena rehearses. Suddenly, the soldiers in the video become rigid and fall into perfect formations. They act in unison, each division performing their tactics with an almost eerie, robotic precision. In the simulation, one unit climbs the trees and then parachutes down, shooting fake guns at all the others on their way to the ground. Another unit appears to dig an underground tunnel to the other side of the forest, emerging from behind and overtaking another group of soldiers.

"Overall," Talina says turning off the video, "battles have become much more effective with the Override. Questions?"

A skinny girl in the front raises her hand timidly.

"What does the Override feel like?" She squeaks.

Talina smiles. "I'm glad you asked." She walks back to the control panel and pushes another button. I jump as the room fills with the sound of blaring horns playing intermittently over a heavy beat. We all look around at each other for a few moments, confused and unsure. Then all at once, I hear Talina's voice in my head.

"Stand up."

There are loud scrapes as everyone stands and pushes back their chair at once.

"Walk to the front, starting on the left foot, in three-seconds. Three, two, one."

My feet move of their own volition. It's the most absurd and unsettling feeling I've ever experienced. I try once or twice not to walk forward, but I am unable to resist. I see now that Talina is speaking into a small microphone that is attached to a conspicuous silver box at her feet.

We converge in the open area at the front of the room, evenly spaced about a foot away from each other.

"Stop."

Talina's voice rings in my head for a moment during the instant of relative silence, and then commands come into my head so quickly, I can barely understand them.

"Turn, right kick, squat down, jump up..."

My body responds faster than my mind can process the commands, and it's making me dizzy. So I stop focusing on Talina's words and try to observe everyone else. We're all dancing. Some look more natural than others, but everyone performs the same moves to the music.

I spot Tristan's sour face a few feet away from me, and I hear him complaining loudly, "This is the dumbest thing I've ever done!" Apparently, Talina heard his comment as well because suddenly everyone else stands still while Tristan twirls wildly like a drunk ballerina.

I laugh, but soon my body is obeying commands again, executing dance moves I've never seen before in my life. The room starts to spin as the music and movements get faster. Just as I'm starting to lose my breath, the music ends and my head clears. I look around and see that we're all lying on our sides with one fist in the air. There is a mixture of laughter, cursing and clapping as people come out of the Override. I feel energized - I've never danced with a group like that before.

"*That* is what it feels like to be overridden," Talina shouts over the noise. "But I can't promise there will always be music." There are a few chuckles as everyone gets to their feet and returns to their chairs. Alia finds me and starts going off about the music, but I'm lost in my own thoughts. That was probably the most fun I've had in a long time. *So why do I feel so disturbed?*

Chapter 10

I am being strangled.

I gasp as I wake up from my nightmare, but when I open my eyes, I see that the dream is real. Tristan is on top of me. I can't breathe, I can't scream, I can't call for help.

"This is awesome! I'm so glad I found you!"

Now I'm confused. As I more fully gain consciousness, I see Tristan's face, but it's softer, and it's surrounded by long, white-blonde hair.

"I had to ask about a dozen people which dorm you were in, and most of them weren't very helpful, but I just had to meet you!"

I sit up. No one is pinning me down. A girl who looks like Tristan is hovering over me. Her mouth looks like it's stained with green Energy capsules. My shock subsides and I can finally get some words out.

"Who are you?"

"Oh! I'm sorry! This must be really weird for you, being woken up by a total stranger! I'm Cassidy Prewitt! I'm Tristan's sister!"

"Twin?" I ask groggily.

"Yes! How did you know?"

I stare at this overactive girl for a few moments, and then around at the other girls in my dorm. Alia is stifling a giggle, but the other four just eye Cassidy wearily. It's still pretty dark outside, I'm guessing we were all woken up by my surprise visitor.

"Anyway," Cassidy continues, not at all put off by my less than friendly demeanor, "I just want to thank you for saving my brother's life. What you did was spectacular! I wish I had the guts to do something like that."

"Well, I'm glad that somebody's happy about it." I reply, trying to summon a smile.

Cassidy beams. "I know he can be a little crazy sometimes, but I'm just so glad he's still alive!" She starts to tear up. I panic. This girl is over the top when she's happy, I'm not eager too see what she's like when she's distressed.

"Well, Cassidy, it was really nice to meet you, but I think I'm going to try to sleep a little bit longer before practical training today," I hint.

"Oh, for sure," Cassidy says cheerily, her tears vanishing, "I should get some sleep too, I've been awake all night!" I watch her take a couple yellow Pacify capsules before she waves goodbye and closes the door.

I fall back on my pillow, smiling. I think Tristan's sister might be his one redeeming quality. I listen as the other girls resume the slow, steady breathing of sleep, but I can't settle down. I toss and turn for a few minutes and consider commanding myself to fall asleep like Joby did, but for some reason I can't bring myself to do it.

Finally I give up and slip out of bed. The clock on the wall across the room tells me it's almost 5:00. I figure I'll just arrive early to the Coliseum. Really early.

It is strangely quiet outside. I can only just barely hear the whir of the massive turbines that keep the barge aloft. After taking a quick shower I make my way to the Coliseum. Being the largest building on the ship, it's pretty easy to find. The massive doors are unlocked, which seems a little odd to me, but I guess they can't have too much trouble with people who have been conditioned to behave. Unless, of course, you're someone like Miles Paxton.

The first thing I notice is the ceiling. It is composed completely of thousands of large, long shards of glass hanging vertically like stalactites. They look so precarious, like they could drop at any moment, and I hesitate to move forward. I take a few moments to observe the expanse of this enclosure which houses a field, a boxing ring, a pool, a weight lifting area, a hover chamber, firing and archery ranges, an urban obstacle course, and likely countless other features I can't see from where I'm standing. Mounted on the wall to the left of me are hundreds of various weapons, ranging from rifles to crossbows to axes. I walk by and marvel at the variety and complexity of these instruments, but also wonder at the endless creativity of those seeking to inflict harm and death. I know these weapons are a great source of defense, but must there be so many ways to hurt someone?

I turn and see what looks like a jungle in the far corner of the Coliseum and cross to see exactly what it is. The floors are springy and I can't resist leaping from one foot to the other, gaining buoyancy with every step. I'm so focused on leaping that once I reach the room I almost run into some low-hanging vines. I realize now that what

I thought was a jungle is a series of loosely looped cables and bent poles. I hear a faint buzzing sound. On a hunch, I pull out a few strands of my hair and drop them on the nearest cable. They burn up on contact. I'll be interested to know what purpose this area serves in our training.

I carefully back away from the electrocution cables and look for something else to explore. I would love to try out some acrobatics in the hover chamber, but there are cameras everywhere, and I really don't want to draw attention to myself. Instead, I settle for a little experimentation. I scoop up a handful of water from the pool, noticing as I carry it that what I spill evaporates immediately when it hits the floor. When I reach the hover room, I only have a little water left, but it's enough that several droplets form and float through the air as I stick my hand through the doorway.

I watch the droplets go off in different directions, no order, no purpose, just drifting whichever way they're carried. It's beautiful, but for some reason it makes me uneasy. I'm considering going back to handle some of the weapons when I hear a loud crash behind me. I spin around and see a young boy staring out at me from behind a bench press.

I saw a rabbit once. It was years ago when I was walking home from school. That was the first and only time I've ever seen an animal. I remember it froze when it saw me, it's glassy eyes large with fear.

This boy reminds me of that rabbit.

He is almost in full view, and doesn't make a move to hide, but it looks like he's trying to cower behind the

72

bench. There are a few weights scattered at his feet, which must have been the cause of the noise. He has curly black hair and an upturned nose. He can't be more than nine years old.

I walk slowly toward him, not sure what exactly I'm going to do when or if I reach him. His eyes grow wide, but he still doesn't move. I'm about 20 feet away from him. A door opens.

"Hey Mari! You trying to show us all up again by being early?" Liam's jovial face appears in the entryway. He's followed by a boy and a girl, who, judging by their size, look like they're also from his compound. They walk forward, oblivious of the young intruder across from me, probably because the curly haired boy is obscured from their view by several hanging heavy bags.

For some inexplicable reason, I'm overcome with an urge to protect this stranger. Maybe because he reminds me of my little brother. I walk quickly toward Liam and point to the wall behind them.

"Hey! Have you guys seen the crossbows yet?" I call out. They all turn around and look at the wall of weapons with obvious interest. I venture a quick glance back and catch a glimpse of the boy running off to a room in the far corner of the Coliseum. I turn back to the group, who are ogling some sort of spear. They're all pretty involved in examining the weapons, so I'm left to my own thoughts, wondering for the second time this week if I've done the right thing.

Chapter 11

We stand in a sloppy semicircle around Talina and Justin, who are giving final instructions and warnings. I've been distracted throughout the whole tour of the Coliseum and explanation of weapons, half expecting that boy to appear again. But if he's managed to stay on the barge undetected this long, he's probably got a good hiding place.

"Justin will be assisting with weapons, should you need supervision," Talina explains. "If you were never shown one or more of these exercises in school, or have simply forgotten, a collection of Adhesives covering every defense can be found in the room to my right." Talina looks around at everyone. "You may begin."

When nobody moves, Justin furrows his eyebrows and yells, "Go!"

The trainees disperse in a dozen different directions, a handful heading off toward the Adhesives for a refresher, or perhaps to postpone actually having to do anything. I really want to try out the hover chamber, but I notice Tristan heading that way, so instead I follow Justin over to the wall of weapons. I see Joby there, staring in awe at some very large guns.

"Can you believe all this stuff?" Joby exclaims when he sees me. "I don't even think I could lift half of these, much less carry them!"

"Maybe you could bring a little wagon into battle with you for your guns," I respond jokingly.

"But then I'd still have to pull something," Joby muses.

I chuckle at his conundrum as I watch Justin walk over and flip on a switch that says: "Training Mode."

"All right," Justin barks, "who's first?"

The dozen or so people who have gathered by the weapons shrink back or look at their feet. *Who's first for what?* I wonder. Talina made it sound like this was a free for all, I didn't think there'd be any formalities. Maybe Justin does things a little differently. I don't want to look like I'm displaying any kind of abnormal bravery, but the lack of participation is killing me.

"I'll go," I announce, walking forward.

"Figures," Justin mutters sarcastically, although I think I see a hint of a smile at the corners of his mouth. "The procedure is simple, just take any weapon off the wall and be prepared to think," he explains. Confused, I move toward a pair of swords. I look back at Justin and all the others watching me, then tentatively lift the two swords away from the wall.

With a screeching sound, the wall splits open and a large figure comes at me, wielding similar swords. I'm frozen in fear. My enemy charges, swords slashing in the air. I start swinging my swords wildly while cowering and trying to protect my face. I'm able to deliver a few good blows to my opponent, but I'm severely outmatched. Over the clanging of metal on metal, I hear Justin yelling:

"Use your Amplifier!"

Of course! What was I thinking? Well, clearly, I wasn't. I back up a few steps and give myself a command.

"Mari, attack the contender using the dual sword technique until he is incapacitated."

The command takes effect immediately. My body runs forward, the swords now moving fluidly through the air. It's almost as if I'm observing myself from somewhere else. I clash with my opponent, attacking and defending like I've done this my whole life. With my fear gone, I'm able to see that I'm fighting against a very lifelike mechanical manikin, the deception only evident in the abnormal facial movements and tell-tale lines at the neck and joints. I find myself face to face with the manikin, struggling against it with our swords locked together in front of us. Suddenly, I fall to the floor, causing the manikin to fall forward and stumble over me. I quickly jump up, spin around, and thrust both of my swords into the manikin's back. The manikin goes still and I regain control of my body.

"Apart from some panicking at the start, she did all right," Justin states to the group behind him, bringing me fully back to reality. "Now you all know more or less what's in store, so get going."

The others step forward and choose weapons, causing the wall to split open in about a dozen different places. They each command themselves and overtake the manikins, some more swiftly than others. One girl takes down her manikin with one fatal throw of an axe, while down the line, a boy with a bow and arrows struggles to hit his mark as he dodges the arrows the dummy is shooting at him. Joby is repeatedly firing a revolver at his advancing manikin, but it does not go down until he shoots it squarely in the head. Apparently, it was wearing a bullet proof vest.

I try out the throwing stars and a massive machine gun that sends jolts through my body when it fires, but I'm intrigued by the bow staffs. Every person that chooses that weapon performs the exact same routine against the opposing manikin. There is no variation. It seems that the Amplifier only has one course of attack with this particular weapon. When it's my turn, I try to change things up a little.

"Mari, attack the opponent with the bow staff and basic acrobatics until he is defeated."

The staff spins flawlessly between my hands as I advance, but right before making contact with the manikin, I dig one end of the staff into the floor and propel myself over the robotic dummy, knocking it soundly on the head as I sail over. Landing on the other side, I do a series of backflips to distance myself, then come at the manikin again, this time planting the staff on his foot and swinging my body around to knock him over. While the manikin tries to reorient itself, I run toward it and once again use the staff to hoist myself into the air, spinning and twisting as I go, and land directly on top of the manikin, plunging the staff into its chest.

That was interesting, I think, standing and pulling the staff out of my fake victim. I'm considering trying another variation, but then I look out and see that everyone in the weapons area is staring at me. Justin is walking briskly in my direction, looking grim. I hurry to return the bow staff to its place, but before I can get there, Justin is grabbing my arm and spitting angry words into my face.

"What was that?" He hisses. His face is so close to mine that a few strands of his long hair brush my cheek.

"I - I'm sorry, I was just experimenting ... just trying something different."

"Different is not equal!" He growls, emphasizing each word by shaking my arm. "Don't ever do anything like that again!"

He releases me and stomps away. People give him a wide berth as he passes. I stand there dumbfounded, massaging the sore spots he left in my arm. I've never been punished for curiosity. It's starting to feel like every aspect of my personality does not belong here.

Chapter 12

The recording room is hidden away in the most remote corner of the barge. It took me almost 45 minutes to find the faded red sign that marked the small enclosure. No wonder families hardly ever hear from their trainees and soldiers.

It's been 3 and a half weeks. I'm already behind on my promise to Daniel. It's not that I haven't had time, we have free hours every now and then and Alia's been spending most of her time with that jerk, Jaren. I guess I just don't have much good news to send home. But I've put it off long enough, so I take a deep breath, sit in the chair, and press the start button. A red light comes on, indicating that I'm being recorded. I have to be convincing, otherwise my mother will know something is wrong.

"Hi mom! Hi Daniel! How are you two?" I start, making an effort to smile. "Sorry I didn't send one of these sooner, I've just been so busy! Training is great and I love being Amplified! We've been learning so many new things, I can hardly keep up! But it's still so exciting! I've made a bunch of new friends and things are going really well. Daniel, I hope you're enjoying school, and mom, I hope everything is going well at the farm. I miss you guys so much and I hope to hear from you soon! Love you!"

I press the stop button and sigh. I think I overdid it, that message was too generic and full of lies. I *have* made a couple friends, and I do enjoy learning and trying out new things with my Amplifier, but mainly I overanalyze all my behavior and try to stay out of the way. But I figure it's better than nothing, so I send 2 Adhesives of the recording to my mom, typing her name and compound number into the Conveyor.

I'm about to leave the recording room, but I feel like someone should know how I really feel, so I sit down again and start another recording.

"Hi Adrian. How are you liking your work rotation? What jobs have you done so far? I'd love to hear all about it." I pause. My older brother wasn't very helpful the last time I confided in him, but I feel like he might be the only person who would understand. "Training has been okay," I continue. "Amplification really is fantastic, but sometimes I feel like I don't fit in here. I keep making mistakes that I never knew were mistakes. Did that ever happen to you? Maybe I'm just being too sensitive. Anyway, I miss you and I hope everything is great. Love ya."

I send the recording off to my brother and smile at the stark difference between the messages. He may not respond, but at least it felt good to get my feelings out in the open.

————-

"Why are we doing this, again?"

"I don't know. They give the order, and I obey."

I listen, amused, at the conversation between two guys in my tagging group. I think their names are Todd and Derek. There are six of us all together; those two, myself, Liam, Joby, and another girl, Hannah, who I don't know very well.

This morning we parachuted from the air barge into the Preserve, a lush, thickly forested area where all the animals in the Community are kept. I can't get over how beautiful it is. I've never seen so much green. It almost makes me dizzy.

"We're tranquilizing and tagging the animals so the Community can keep track of them," Liam announces matter-of-factly, interrupting Todd and Derek's banter.

"Why do they need to keep track of them?" Derek asks, almost tripping over a tree root.

"For nutrition, mainly," Liam replies smoothly. "The Community needs to keep track of their health and reproduction so that our supply stays constant."

"Wait," Hannah interjects, "you mean the capsules are made from animals?"

"Sure, a few of them," Liam says simply. "But it's such a minuscule amount it really doesn't deplete the animal reserves by too much."

I shiver. I always knew the animals were used for capsules, and Liam talks about them nonchalantly enough, but knowing that I'm about to encounter something that I eat just makes me feel weird. Not that it should change anything, it just seems a little surreal.

"Gross," Hannah blurts, "I'm not eating those capsules ever again."

"Ah, you'll get over it soon enough," Liam counters.

We follow our maps to our designated tagging area. Todd had offered to do the navigating for the group, but we all ended up using our own Amplifiers to find our way instead. No need to work together when everyone is capable of doing it themselves. We climb over some large rocks and come to a clearing. Liam and Joby stop to take some Hydration capsules, so I check my supplies one more time. It's all still there: two loaded tranquilizer guns, a dozen metal ear tags, a scanner, some Nutrition and Hydration capsules, and a few flares in case of emergency.

We continue on through the trees, following a river and steadily climbing higher. I keep hearing Liam command himself to keep walking. I guess this hike would be pretty difficult for someone who isn't used to physical activity. Finally, we turn a corner and are facing the biggest waterfall I've ever seen. At least it looks bigger than any of the ones I've seen in pictures. And surrounding the pool at the base of the falls are a dozen different animals.

"Ok, ok, so wait," Joby sputters, almost hyperventilating, "do we scan the animal first and then tranquilize it? Or do we tag it and then scan it? Or do we — "

"Slow down, rookie," Derek cuts in, "don't worry about it — it's all in your head. Just use your Amplifier!"

"Oh, right," Joby says sheepishly, turning to focus on the animal nearest him.

I look over at something large with horns and give myself the command:

"Mari, tranquilize and tag the animal."

My hand goes to the gun almost robotically. I take aim and hit the beast just below its shoulder. It takes a few unsteady steps and then falls to the ground. I approach the furry heap. The scanner identifies it as a male Elk, and also lists its weight, age, and diet. I insert a metal tag into the scanner and it comes out engraved with this information. I remove the old tag from the elk's ear and clip the new one into its place.

We continue this process until all the animals are unconscious and newly tagged. I walk around to look at the animals; a couple more elk, some deer, an antelope, a moose, and two buffalo. I pause at the last buffalo, amazed at its huge head.

"It's beautiful, isn't it?"

For a split-second I think the buffalo is talking to me. Then I realize Joby is behind me. I look again at the buffalo and shrug.

"Yeah, I guess so. In a hairy, brutish kind of way..."

"No," Joby laughs, "I'm talking about this place! The trees, the sky, the waterfall ... it's kind of romantic."

I take a deep breath and admire the scenery. It really is stunning.

"It's gorgeous," I admit, trying to take in the magnitude of the waterfall all at once. I turn around and notice that Joby is uncomfortably close to me and that his eyes are oddly intense. I look around for everyone else and see that they're all far away on the other side of the pool. I start to panic.

"Mari," Joby says, leaning toward me, "we've been friends for a while, and lately I've just felt that-" he stops short, examining my face. "Mari, are you okay?"

I'm not okay. I was uneasy before, but now I am simply terrified. A massive animal with sharp teeth and giant claws has appeared behind Joby. I slowly lift the scanner in my hand to identify the beast. Black bear.

The bear charges before I have time to command myself or reach for my tranquilizer gun. I grab Joby and we dive sideways to the ground, out of the path of the attacking creature. The bear runs past us, but turns quickly and starts to pursue again. We get up and start running, but the bear is close behind and closing the gap. I'm frantically trying to get my tranquilizer gun, but it keeps getting jostled around in my pack.

"We've got to split up!" I yell to Joby. There's no use in both of us being killed. Joby nods his head, but looks worried. The trees are starting to thicken. "Ready?" I shout, taking a quick glance behind me at the bear a few feet away. "Now!"

We run in different directions, Joby goes into the trees while I scramble up some rocks. It seems the bear is momentarily confused, but then repositions and starts heading after me. I slow down to find my tranquilizer gun, thinking I've put enough distance between us, but when I twist around to shoot, the bear is nearly on top of me. It claws at my arm, knocking the gun to the ground and sending searing pain through my body. I stumble and try to get away, but the bear keeps swatting at me. I lose my balance and fall. I am completely vulnerable.

84

The bear hovers over me, snapping its jaws inches from my face. I can't breathe, I can't find my voice to try to command myself, so in desperation I start kicking the bear as hard and fast as I can. I feel flesh being torn from my leg, but I keep kicking. Aggravated, the bear backs away and rises up on its hind legs. I know it's going to come at me again, and I know this time it will probably kill me.

I take a deep breath. *I guess a bear attack isn't the worst way to die.* But then the bear stops and gives an odd growl. The fury leaves its eyes and a few seconds later it collapses forward onto my legs. Behind where the bear was standing is Liam, holding his tranquilizer gun aloft and looking victorious, although his hands are shaking slightly.

"Are you all right?" He asks, rushing toward me. I'm struggling to free my legs and Liam shoves the bear back as much as he can so I can pull myself away. "We saw it come over the ridge but we were too far away to warn you guys," he explains quickly. "Luckily, you ran back in our direction. Otherwise, I would have never made it to you in time."

"That is lucky," I say weakly. I attempt to stand, but something is wrong with my left leg and it won't hold my weight. I stumble forward and Liam catches me.

"Wow, Mari, you're pretty beat up," Liam says, looking me over and draping my arm over his shoulders. "Let's get you back to the barge."

"Thanks, Liam," I mutter gratefully.

I let myself be half-dragged by Liam back to the waterfall. The rest of our group rushes forward when they see us nearing the pool. I'm glad to see that Joby is with them and safe, but he's looking at me with a strange expression. I feel something stinging. I look down at my leg and immediately wish I hadn't. Liam is using the water from the pool to clean a grotesque, bloody gash on my left thigh. I cringe and squeeze Liam's arm. He says something soothing, but I cant tell what it is.

Suddenly, the rest of the group erupts into laughter.

"Liam," Todd chokes out, "you weigh three-hundred and fifteen pounds?"

I manage to look back and see that they're all crowded around Joby's scanner, which is pointed at Liam. Liam turns bright red.

"Sorry," Joby mumbles, "it was an accident."

I'm nearly delirious, but I don't think it was an accident.

Chapter 13

I wake up to bright lights and a dozen pairs of eyes staring at me. I jerk to sit up, but something is restraining my body. From somewhere behind me I hear Talina's voice.

"Often victims can be confused or frantic when they regain consciousness, so it's usually a good idea to strap them down."

I glance around to try to make sense of this eerie situation. Everyone is wearing white, sterile jackets, and Talina is in the corner, gesturing to an image of an injured body on a large screen. *My body!* I'm hardly wearing any clothes and I have cuts and gashes on my arms, legs, and stomach. The last thing I remember is the bear attack and being taken to the air barge. I must have passed out. I writhe to free myself, but I'm held securely by two thick straps across my chest and hips. My fellow trainees look at me with dull interest, and then back to something Talina is showing them.

"Here we see the victim has a broken ankle, which is something we can treat, but ultimately cannot heal," Talina explains. "However, these other cuts and this infected wound are relatively easy to fix if you know the correct commands. Let's start with this cut on her right forearm. Any volunteers?"

I can't believe it! I think. *They're studying me!* I feel nauseous. A boy is approaching with a medical bag, apparently the first "volunteer."

"Gordon," he says evenly, "clean, sterilize, and bandage the injury." He opens the bag and pulls out the appropriate items, then busies himself with disinfecting the cut on my arm. It burns, but I will myself not to scream. When he's finished, I have a tidy bandage covering the cut.

"Nicely done, Gordon," Talina praises. "There's a deep cut down here on her calf. Justine, would you like to address this one?"

Justine steps forward, medical bag in hand.

"Justine, clean, sterilize and stitch the wound."

Stitch? *Stitch?* Amplifier or not, I don't know that I can put my trust in a 15 year old stranger to stitch me up. I watch in horror as she numbs my calf and begins to thread the sutures through my skin. I don't feel much pain, but my skin still crawls at the sight of it. After what seems like an eternity, she finishes and cleans up the area. I think I might pass out.

"Thank you, Justine," Talina says as Justine walks back to the other trainees. "Now, one of the most pressing concerns on the victim's body is this large gash on the thigh, which is clearly infected," Talina lectures as she points to my thigh on the screen. "Because of the infection, we will likely have to remove flesh and pieces of bone to prevent it from spreading."

And with that pronouncement, I decide I've had enough. I've been lying here, nearly naked, while they have used me to practice their surgery skills. There is no way they are going to cut into my bone. While everyone is focused on the screen, I give myself a discreet, yet clear command.

"Mari, find a way to remove these binding straps and get off this table."

For the first time, I feel the Amplifier activate my mind, which is exhilarating and terrifying all at once. Everything is sharper. I glance around and notice things that might be useful: some tweezers, a scalpel, a pen. I finally focus on a small surgical saw in the pocket of Talina's sterile jacket.

I make a gagging sound, as if I'm about to vomit. Talena stops her instruction and walks over to me.

"Mari, what's wrong?" She asks, a slight edge in her voice.

"I- I- I- can't..." I choke out in a whisper. As expected, Talena leans closer, trying to make out what I'm saying. In one quick movement, I grab the saw from her pocket and bring it down to slice through the strap across my hips. Someone moves forward to restrain me, but I swing my legs across and kick them to the floor. The momentum of my legs causes the table I'm still strapped on to tip over sideways, but now the strap is loose on my upper shoulder, so I'm able to free that arm enough to cut through my chest strap.

I push the table away and stand to face a room of shocked trainees. I limp a few feet toward the door, then promptly pass out.

———-

When I wake up the second time, I'm in the same room, but now I'm alone with Talina. Her back is to me. It looks like she's cleaning up some surgical equipment. I realize I'm not strapped to the table, but something tells me I shouldn't try to escape again. I gingerly lift my leg and see that the infected gash on my thigh has been cleaned and bandaged. At least I was unconscious when the pieces of bone were being removed.

"That was quite the stunt you pulled," Talina comments without turning around. I don't know how she knew I was awake. "I'm starting to think you don't like being restricted," she jokes, finally turning to face me. She has a cut above her eyebrow. *Did I do that?* I think. I can't remember. "Mari, you're not an easy one to control."

Talina looks at me expectantly, but I have no response. I sit up on the table slowly. I'm anticipating another lecture, or a dismissal, or worse. So I'm surprised by what she says next.

"Listen, Mari," she begins regretfully, "I'm sorry I used you to instruct the others. It just seems like it's more effective when there's a live victim, and these things are especially important now, considering..." she trails off, staring at a point above my head. I decide not to press this cryptic issue that's making Talina act so ... sensitive. Instead, I change the subject.

"So, I'm not in trouble?"

"No," Talina replies, snapping out of her thoughts. "I should have known not to use you for a subject of study."

She gives me a strained smile. There's an odd silence for a few moments. I consider leaving, but something's been bothering me.

"Before, when I cut myself off the table, something weird happened."

"Let me guess," Talina interjects, "you used your Amplifier for critical thinking."

"Yeah, I guess I did."

Talina sighs. "That is a brilliant but potentially dangerous feature of the Amplifiers which should be used sparingly. Whenever you allow the Amplifier to access your brain, you're giving it complete control. You lose yourself — doing whatever it takes to achieve your goal, regardless of your morals or allegiances. People have quite literally lost their minds by giving themselves over too frequently to their Amplifiers."

"Oh, ok," I reply feebly. Suddenly the boldness I felt at freeing myself earlier now seems like complete idiocy. It felt amazing to have my mind and senses heightened, but I don't like the thought of being manipulated.

Sensing that it's time for me to leave, I get down from the table, only to nearly collapse when I try to stand on my broken ankle. There is a bandage around my foot, likely something else Talina did while I was unconscious.

"Healing your ankle will take a little bit of courage, and it will be very painful," Talina says nonchalantly as she hands me a pair of crutches.

"What do you mean?" I ask.

"Anytime you command your body to speed up the process of healing, it's going to be a little ... uncomfortable," Talina explains.

It doesn't sound like the most pleasant experience, but my curiosity gets the better of me. I try to recall everything I have learned about the body, and hope I say the right thing.

"Mari, rejoin and fuse the broken bones in your left ankle."

Excruciating pain courses through my leg. I grip the side of the table to keep myself from collapsing. I fervently wish I had not given myself this command. My knuckles are white on the table and I just want to detach my leg from my body to rid myself of this agony. Seconds feel like hours. Then all at once, the sharp pain leaves and all I feel is a dull ache. Exhausted, I fall forward onto the table, feeling like I could probably sleep for three days.

"Well, you certainly took the express route on that one," Talina observes. "Next time, you might want to take your body through the appropriate stages instead of going straight to the finish line."

I grunt a reply. Talina gathers her things and walks out of the room, leaving me alone and slumped halfway on the table. When the door closes, I slide down to the floor. The hard tile feels cool on my sweating forehead. I lie there for several hours until I'm finally able to get up and stumble back to my dorm.

Chapter 14

"Mari! What are you listening to?"

I look around and realize that Janet, one of my dorm mates, is yelling at me. She's probably been asking me this question over and over, but I haven't been able to hear her. I stop the music on my device and pull the wires out of my ears.

"Sorry Janet, I couldn't hear you," I say sheepishly. "It's just some ancient music, do you want to listen to it?"

"What does it sound like?"

"Here, listen for yourself," I say, handing her the device. She looks it over for a moment, then cautiously holds the wires to her ears. She listens for a little while, then hands the device back to me.

"I like it," she confesses, "but it makes me feel kind of ... weird."

I shrug and take the device back from her. The old music usually inspires me, but I guess it might seem strange to someone hearing it for the first time.

"Some of us are going to hang out in the Coliseum, do you want to come?" Janet asks, hopping off her bed.

"No thanks, I think I'll just relax in here."

"Okay, see you later," Janet calls as she walks out.

The past few days it seems I've been spending a lot of time alone. I took an entire day to rest after the bear attack, and since then I haven't felt like being around people. I'll go to training and practice sessions, but during any free time I stay in my dorm.

I go back to listening to my ancient device, right now I really don't want to think about anything. A movie Adhesive would probably be more effective in distracting me from my conflicting thoughts, but I don't feel like going to get one.

A slow, pulsating song is starting to put me to sleep when suddenly the music abruptly cuts off and I hear a voice speaking from my device.

"Mari, you have to get out of here. You're better than this, you shouldn't resign yourself to a life of Amplified enslavement."

I sit straight up in bed. While the words, intensity and general intrusion on my privacy are all alarming, what agitates me the most is the voice. *I know that voice.* But I can't place it. More than anything, I want to know who belongs to that voice.

"... you may think there is safety and prestige in the Amplifiers, but there are forces at work that are so much bigger than being able to do a few tricks. Mari, use your head. Remember where you come from. Get out before it's too late."

And just as suddenly as it came, the voice is gone and the music resumes. I rewind and replay the song over and over, but I cannot find the message again.

I lay back in bed, perplexed and confused. Who would go to such lengths to warn and threaten me? Is this a trick? Is someone here trying to scare me away from Training? But then there was that voice. A voice that comforts and haunts me at the same time. Not knowing who's voice it was is driving me crazy.

"Hey Mari! Stop lying around and come party with us!"

I just about fall out of my bed as Alia comes running up to me, shouting loudly and excitedly. She stops short when she sees my face.

"Mari, what happened? You look terrified!"

I hesitate. I should tell Alia about this, but I haven't quite processed it yet. I want to keep it to myself for a little while.

"Oh, it's nothing. I think I just got startled when you came in," I lie.

"Are you sure?" Alia presses. "I've never seen you look like that before."

I attempt a smile. I realize there's only one easy way out of this.

"Yeah, I'm fine," I tell her, "I've probably just been spending too much time by myself lately. Let's go to that party."

"Really?" Alia exclaims, immediately brightening. "Great! Let's go!"

With Alia effectively distracted from my crisis, we head off to the recreation lounge. According to Alia, this party is so amazing it'll change my life. But all I can think about is that voice.

————-

There are only about 30 people in the recreation lounge, but they're so boisterous, it seems like there are a lot more. Everyone is practically screaming to be heard

95

over the too-loud music. Several couples are wrestling playfully in the trampoline rooms, and it's a little jarring to suddenly see so much physical interaction between them.

Alia takes me straight to Jaren, who is surrounded by a bunch of other trainees.

"Alia, baby, did you have to bring your stupid friend along?" Jaren complains. I don't make any effort to hide my disgust.

"Aw, come on, Jaren," Alia teases, "she'll loosen up after you give her some."

"All right, fine," He responds reluctantly. He reaches into a large bag and holds out a few purple and lime green capsules. Intoxication.

"Where did you get those?" I demand, taking a quick step back from the dangerous capsules.

"I found them in my dorm, what's it to you?" Jaren snaps, putting the capsules back in his bag.

"We're in the one place where they're forbidden," I retort. "Don't you think an entire bag of them just laying around is a little suspicious?"

"Lighten up, Mari," Alia prompts, trying to calm the tension between me and Jaren.

"Whatcha gonna do, *clam*, tattle on us?" Jaren sneers, but I can tell he's a little paranoid.

"No," I answer, "I think letting you all be useless idiots for the night is punishment enough."

I walk away from Jaren, Alia, and the rest of the group. I hear them talking about me, but I don't care. I've had plenty of experience being the weird one and it's starting to affect me less and less. I find an empty trampoline room and lie down on the resilient floor. Maybe I *am* overreacting. Maybe it's just a coincidence that means some of the trainees can have a little bit of fun. But I can't get past the fact that a bag of Intoxication capsules, one of the only things that shuts of our Amplifiers, mysteriously found its way into Jaren's hands.

"Mari! I agree with you!"

Cassidy's eager face appears in front of mine. I'm lucky my instinct was to roll away rather than to sit up, otherwise we'd both have quite a headache.

"Hi Cassidy, how are you?" I ask warily. She has the familiar, green Energy-capsule tinge around her mouth, but now, in addition to her hyperactivity, she has the glazed and unfocused look of someone who's heavily intoxicated. I really don't mind Tristan's sister, but I don't know if I can handle her intensity right now.

"I'm great!" She replies, "I just feel fuzzy!" She's jumping all over the place, literally bouncing off the walls. "But I was listening to what you said to Jaren, and it makes complete sense! Someone's probably trying to sabotage us!" She finishes in a cheerful tone that doesn't at all match the intent of her words. I manage a smile. She might not be the first person I'd pick to have on my side, but her loyalty is endearing.

"Thanks Cassidy, I really appreciate that you -"

"And you know what?" Cassidy interrupts, "I think I know where those capsules came from."

"Yeah?"

"Yeah! Every once in a while I see this little guy creeping around the Coliseum. Sometimes I think I'm hallucinating, so I never told anybody about him, but now I'm pretty sure he's real. He's probably the one who put those capsules in Jaren's dorm room."

"What does he look like?" I ask, hoping it's the same boy I saw that early morning in the Coliseum and not a figment of her imagination.

"He's really young and has curly, dark hair, and a birthmark on his neck."

"Where do you usually see him?"

"Back by the urban obstacle course. I tried to follow him a couple times, but I can never figure out where he goes."

I get to my feet, feeling a sense of purpose for the first time in a week.

"Thanks Cassidy!" I yell as I run out of the trampoline room. I look around the lounge for Alia to tell her where I'm going, but she and Jaren have disappeared. It's just as well, she probably won't miss me anyway.

I move as quickly as I can to the Coliseum, limping a bit because my ankle is still sore. It's a long shot, but I'm hoping I can get some answers. Somehow I think that this strange stowaway boy and the message I heard on my device earlier are linked.

Chapter 15

The Coliseum appears to be empty, but I keep hearing a continuous squeaking sound. I look around until I finally see some movement in the back corner. Squinting, I can barely make out the figure of Liam on a stationary bicycle, which is a slightly comical sight — he's almost twice the size of the bike. I walk over to see why he's still here.

"Having fun going nowhere fast?" I joke. Liam grins with effort, but a moment later his expression turns to a grimace.

"It's not much fun," he admits, "but I've got to get this done."

"Get what done?"

"This," he states, grabbing his gut. "It's just gotten to the point where I'm tired of being the fattest one here," he explains with a hint of bitterness.

"And how long is that going to take?"

"Well, I've got a program planned out for the next three days. No sleep, no rest, just pure exercise."

"Three days?"

"Yep. Talina even excused me from training, and she told me how to manipulate my metabolism."

"Liam, you're going to kill yourself," I protest, clearly concerned.

"Nope. I commanded myself not to die."

"Ok..." I say uncertainly, wondering if that would even work. I notice a bucket full of capsules on the floor next to him. I peek in. "What, no Pleasure?" I ask.

"No more Pleasure capsules for me," Liam responds, struggling to talk through his heavy breathing," I commanded myself to hate Pleasure."

"I hope not *all* pleasure," I offer feebly, realizing that Liam is really not in the mood for jokes.

"Just the capsules," he says curtly, hinting that he's ready to be done talking.

"Ok," I sigh, "good luck." I leave him panting and cursing on the bike, and make a mental note to check on him over the next few days. I wonder again about the Amplifier's ability to alter your personality. If Liam can make himself hate Pleasure capsules, what else is possible?

When I reach the urban obstacle course, I can barely hear the distant squeak of Liam's bicycle. I gaze at the various cement walls and tangle of pipes and rods. I don't know where to start. *Where would be a good place to hide?* I wonder. I scan the top of the course, and see that one of the pipes seems to go into the ceiling. I just need to figure out how to get up there.

"Mari," I command myself, "reach the uppermost pipe by utilizing the present obstacles and your body."

As if coming to life, my body runs full speed toward a wall. I'm thinking I might smack right into it, but instead I run up the wall, then jump to another one perpendicular to it. I hop back and forth up the walls until I'm on top of one, running along the narrow precipice. I make a long jump from one wall to the next. My head is reeling, but my body stays in full control. I grab onto a rod and swing myself up to a set of upside-down stairs, which I free climb until I reach the highest pipe.

It takes a moment to catch my breath and reorient myself. I've never been afraid of heights, but I feel a little queasy when I look down and see all the many objects I could impale myself on. I shake my head to try to clear the thoughts running through my imagination, concentrating instead on the pipe in front of me. It does go up to the ceiling, and there is a narrow opening that a small person, or a little boy, could probably fit through.

"Mari, climb the pipe."

My amplifier takes over again. My arms grab the sides of the pipe and I shimmy up to the top. The opening is very narrow, and I barely squeeze through. It's dark and dusty in the ceiling, and I'm wishing I had brought a light. My eyes start adjusting to the dimness, and I see there's only enough room to crawl. It's slightly less dusty to the left, so I decide to head that way.

There are a few signs that someone might have crawled through here lately; less cobwebs, a few broken capsule pieces — but I'm still unsure if I'm on the right track. Suddenly, I come upon an open space to my right and see him. For a split second we stare at one another. *He* does *have a birthmark on his neck.* The next moment he scampers back and climbs into one of several smaller tunnels leading away from the open space.

I crawl after him, but I'm too slow. I can see that the tunnel he escaped into leads to a dead end, but it's so small I don't dare climb into it. I'll just have to try to talk to him from here.

"Hey! Who are you and what are you doing here?" I call up the tunnel. All I hear in response is some shuffling. "I know you can hear me!" I taunt. Still nothing. "That's okay, I can wait."

I glance around. The space is about 30 square feet and there are a few pillows and stray capsules scattered on the fragile floor. It's well ventilated thanks to the tunnels, but that might be the only feature that makes the otherwise uninhabitable area decent.

After a few minutes I start to realize that this kid probably has far more experience than me with holing up and waiting it out in unpleasant places, so I try another tactic.

"Listen, I've seen you before. I didn't tell anyone about you then, and I won't tell anyone about you now. I just have some personal questions I want to ask you." After a few moments I add: "and I won't ask you anything that could get you in trouble," hoping it's not a lie.

Besides a muffled cough and a few scratching noises, the boy is silent. After about 15 minutes, I figure he's not going to give in so I start to leave. Then I hear a small voice echo down from the tunnel.

"Are you Mari Quillen?"

"Yes!" I respond quickly. I'm a little disturbed that he knows my name, but I'm eager to keep him talking. His next question comes after some hesitation.

"Did you really save someone from falling off the air barge before you were Amplified?"

Now I'm the one that hesitates. Some of the trainees here are still suspicious of me.

"I did, but I-"

"Wow! That's amazing! How did you know what to do?"

"I didn't. I just ... followed my instinct."

"Well, everyone in the Community is talking about it. Most people don't think it's true."

"What?" I exclaim, a little too loudly. "How do they know?"

"Things like that don't happen very often, so it gets around."

This bit of information puts me on edge. I don't like the thought of a bunch of strangers discussing me. No wonder Governor Plenaris thought it necessary to pay a personal visit. He wanted to keep unusual circumstances like me in line.

"What's your name?" I ask, wanting to change the subject. The boy surprises me by emerging from the tunnel, his face appearing first.

"I'm Felix," he replies, extending his hand to me before he's fully out of the tunnel. We shake hands awkwardly and he sits in front of me, almost like a toddler waiting to hear a story. I guess he's warmed up to me now that he knows who I am.

"How long have you been here?" I say, beginning my interrogation.

"18 days."

"How did you get on the barge?"

"I climbed the cables when they were doing maintenance."

I think back and remember that day. They had to land the barge at one of the maintenance stations. Felix must have known they would be there in advance.

"Did you leave Intoxication capsules in someone's dorm room?"

"Yes."

"Why?"

He grins impishly and shakes his head. He's not going to answer that question.

"Fine," I concede. "Who left that recording on my device?"

Felix scrunches up his face, apparently contemplating whether or not he's going to divulge that information. Suddenly there's a loud clanging sound below us. Felix snaps his head to the side and jumps into another one of the small tunnels, disappearing into the darkness. I move over to the tunnel he went through. I can't see anything, but from the air flow I can guess that there's a way out on the other end. I've lost him.

Frustrated, I crawl out of the ceiling and back down the obstacle course. Liam is now hurling huge weights at an elastic wall and dodging them when they bounce back. I glare at him as I pass. He's probably responsible for the crash that scared Felix away. But deep down I know it's my fault - I should have asked about the recording first.

Chapter 16

Justin is halfway through his safety speech when Alia comes into the Coliseum. Her eyes are red and swollen and her hair is a mess. Now that I think about it, I never saw her come back to the dorm last night. She walks quickly over to the group, her head down, and stands next to me and Joby. Justin studies her for a moment, then resumes his speech.

"Are you all right?" I whisper once everyone has stopped staring.

"I'm fine," she bites back.

I raise my eyebrows at her, but she continues to stare angrily at the floor. Whatever happened last night, she's clearly going to keep it to herself. For a moment, it looks like Joby is going to try to comfort her. He raises his hand and lets it hover by her shoulder, but then he abandons his intent and retracts his hand awkwardly.

People around me start shuffling, and I realize Justin has finished his speech and dismissed everyone. Alia quickly goes to the Adhesive room, not saying a word to either of us.

"Hey, what's Liam doing?" Joby asks me. I follow his gaze over to the pool where Liam appears to be doing intense water aerobics. He looks pretty ridiculous, actually.

"He's exercising himself to death," I respond. "I guess he got permission from Talina to skip out on regular training so he could work out for 3 days straight."

"Oh." Joby mutters, looking a little somber. "He told you that?"

Joby's been acting weird ever since the bear attack. I know what it's about, but I just don't want to address it. Ever.

"Yeah, I ran into him last night," I say impassively. "So what are you going to train on today?"

Joby looks glad for the change of subject and I'm relieved he takes the bait.

"Probably more weapons, I hear they just got new nunchucks. What about you?"

"I'm going to try out the hover chamber."

"Hey, I haven't tried that yet. Maybe I'll come with you."

"Really? I thought I saw you in there last week."

Joby hesitates. He knows I've called his bluff.

"Oh yeah, you're right," He says, reddening slightly. "Guess I forgot." Joby gives me a small smile, then hurries off to the weapons wall.

A surly looking girl appears to be guarding the door to the hover room. I try to get past her, but she stands in my way.

"You have to wait for the next match," she informs me. I look around her into the room and see 4 people grappling with each other in the air.

"What's the point?" I ask her.

"Get everyone else to touch the ground."

It seems like a simple task, but as I watch the mess of bodies as they flail at each other with perfectly executed hits and kicks while getting nowhere, I realize this is going to take a little more mental prowess than the Amplifier can offer. Or at least more than I'm willing to give it.

"So, are you like, the all-time champ?" I ask her.

"No," she responds, confused.

"Did you make up the rules?"

"No, why?"

"I was just wondering what you did to earn the honor of monitoring this room."

"Jaren put me in charge."

"Of course he did," I say bitterly. I scan the Coliseum and spot him on the field, flirting with a tall, dark-haired girl. I guess this might be the reason Alia is so upset. On top of being angry at him for hurting my friend, I'm also indignant that he thinks he can control other people. I'm fighting the urge to go over and punch him in the throat when I hear the girl talking to me.

"Hey, you can go in now."

I turn around to see three disgruntled trainees pulling themselves out of the room, followed by a muscular guy who looks really pleased with himself. *Well, so much for learning from their strategy,* I think as I glide into the room. There are two boys and another girl hovering closely together and talking to one another, but they stop abruptly when I enter. Looks like they're planning to take me out first.

"You have one minute to adjust before the match begins," the guard girl calls from the entrance.

I float around almost helplessly in the air. I notice that I can maneuver slowly in a chosen direction by

107

mimicking swimming motions, but not very effectively. I survey the area, trying to find anything I can use to my advantage. It's pretty sparse. There are some bars on the ceiling and some kind of panel on the far wall, but for the most part it looks like propelling myself from the walls is going to be my best option for any kind of attack. The other three have formed a cluster together on one of the corners near the ceiling. I move to the corner farthest from them.

"Ready?" The question that sounds more like a command echoes from the entrance. "Begin!"

My three aggressors lunge at me, their combined weight allowing them to move more quickly across the room. They each give themselves a different command, but I can't quite tell who is saying what.

"Chase, punch her is the stomach."

"Melody, detach her from the wall."

"Aaron, kick her to the ground."

Great. Weaken me, take away my defenses, and force me to the ground. A simple, yet effective plan. I close my eyes and brace myself for the barrage of pain coming my way, but to my surprise, I feel only the slight graze of a foot across my back. I look up and see that the group has lost momentum, the anti-gravity rendering their commands almost useless. There is no force behind their actions. I almost laugh as I grab onto their bodies and pull myself up above them.

"Mari, flip up and push straight down off the ceiling," I command. The flip is slow and deliberate, but is executed nonetheless. I kick firmly off the ceiling and land on the group that attempted to attack me, pushing them all down toward the floor. But my push looses steam and only the boy on the bottom of the pile touches the ground. He stares hatefully at me before leaving the room.

Before I can revel in my small victory, the other two are grabbing at me and pulling me down to get themselves to a better position. Now beneath them, they both kick at me, inching me downward. A severe kick to my right shoulder sends me spinning out of their range. I'm lucky to be away from them for the moment, but my shoulder is throbbing. I reach the opposite wall and try desperately to anchor myself there, but there's nothing to hold on to. The girl comes flying above me and I can see that she's going to copy my maneuver of pushing off the ceiling to get me down to the ground. I watch her carefully, trying to stay as close as I can to the wall. She propels herself off the ceiling and is coming at me fast. I wait until right before she reaches me to push against the wall and move out of her path. She's moving too quickly to stop herself and she crashes straight into the floor.

Now there's just the other boy left. I'm in a fairly helpless position, floating in the middle of the room, while the boy is holding onto some bars on the ceiling. I twist around to face him, only to receive a nasty kick in the face. I'm sent reeling backwards, my legs coming up over my head. I must be bleeding because I see little red droplets suspended in the air around me. He kicks me again in the hip, which sets me upright. When I see his foot come at me again, I grab onto it and swing myself up to the ceiling, securing myself on one of the bars.

The boy sneers at me menacingly. He's stronger than most of the trainees here and much bigger than me. He comes at me by swinging across the bars. I have to think fast.

"Mari, kick him in the jaw."
Anchored on the bars, my whole body tenses as I swing my legs up and connect a foot to his face. It's a solid kick, but it doesn't do much to deter him. He wraps his legs around me and jerks me down. One of my hands is pulled from the bars, and I'm dangling precariously from the other bar. The boy jerks my body down with his legs again and I'm detached from the ceiling. His pull was so forceful that I'm able to swing beneath him and hook my feet into the bars on the other side of him.

His next move surprises me. He was in prime position to kick the crap out of my face, but I guess that's not the point of the match. He commands himself discreetly, all I can make out is his name: Aaron. He releases the bars and pushes away from the ceiling, then grabs my arms and wrenches me out of my foot holds. We're both in the middle of the room now, and inexplicably, he's swinging me upwards. I don't catch on to his plans until he steers me toward the floor and then swings me back up again. I'm gaining momentum as he spins me around. I have to figure out how to get out of his grip before he throws me to the floor.

He's swinging me so fast that my legs are virtually useless, but I realize that I can probably do some damage with my hands. I grab his forearms and twist them sharply inward. He screams in pain and lets go of me. I'm being hurled downward, but at an angle. I spread my body out as much as possible to slow my descent and level inches from the ground. Already I can hear him coming after me again.

I turn around and push off the wall just as he slams into the spot where I was. He grabs at my feet, but I kick his hands away. As I'm floating past the wall, I catch a glimpse of a switch with a label below it that reads: "RESTORE GRAVITY."

That might be my only chance at winning, I think. This guy is bigger and stronger than me and seems relentless - I don't think I can beat him with sheer force of will. I twist around to double back to the switch. It's high enough on the wall that I can probably hold onto one of the ceiling bars and still reach it with my foot. Aaron is coming at me fast. I grip onto a bar with one hand and grope for the switch with my foot. He's almost reached me when I finally feel my foot connect with the switch and push it downwards. I almost lose my hold on the bar as my fingers suddenly absorb the weight of my body. At the same time, Aaron falls out of the air and smacks abruptly into the floor.

"What was that?" He yells up at me angrily.

"I turned off the anti-gravity," I respond simply.

"That's cheating! You can't do that!" He fumes, struggling to get to his feet.

"I don't recall any rules." I try to keep my voice even, but the truth is he's scaring me a little. I look for the girl who was guarding the door for some back-up, but she's gone. Actually, everyone around the chamber is gone.

"This isn't over," Aaron threatens. He glares at me for a few seconds, then limps out the door.

I exhale. *Why do I always have to win? Why can't I just give up every once in a while?* After a little effort, I find the switch with my foot again and turn the anti-gravity back on. Once again, I am weightless. I give myself a small push away from the wall and float to the entrance of the chamber. My body is aching and my nose is still bleeding.

There's a lot of cheering and shouting coming from across the Coliseum. Mostly everyone is crowded around the boxing ring where it looks like Talina and Justin are giving some kind of demonstration. From where I stand in front of the hover chamber, it's hard to tell exactly what moves they're doing. Not only are they far away, but they're moving so fast. They attack and dodge each other almost at the same time, like a violent, synchronized dance.

"Evan, strangle her."

I hear the voice behind me but don't fully process my danger until a pair of big hands clamp around my neck and pull me back into the hover room. I try to yell for help, but I can't get anything in or out of my throat. It feels surreal to be drifting aimlessly through the air while being strangled. I can't see who my attacker is, but I'm fairly certain there are no trainees here named Evan. In my desperation to breathe I reach back and pull out a

112

chunk of his hair. Blonde strands float past my face. He grunts, but his grip around my neck stays strong.

I'm starting to see spots and I'm fading fast. I start thrashing my arms and legs, but it doesn't do any good. *This guy is going to kill me*. Just before I pass out, I hear him say: "Watch yourself, Miss Quillen."

When I regain consciousness, I'm gasping for air. No more than a couple of minutes could have passed, I can still hear the noise from the boxing ring. My strangler has disappeared, and I'm suspended in the air near one of the corners of the chamber. I feel like death.

I float slowly toward the ceiling and hold loosely onto one of the bars. I have no idea who that guy was or why he attacked me, much less why he then decided not to kill me, and I realize that I don't much care at the moment. I just want to curl up and cry. And I do.

I feel my resolve ebb away as I sob harder and harder. I cry as I recount all of the insane events of the past several weeks, letting out all the emotions I've kept pent up for the sake of appearing strong. I don't care who hears or sees me, I just want to sob until I'm numb. But nobody comes. My tears float away from me and slowly dissolve into the air.

Chapter 17

"These came for you," Alia mumbles sullenly when I walk into our dorm. She's laying face down on her bed and gesturing lazily to some items on the table. From one glance I know what they are, and I hastily grab up the two precious Adhesives from my mother and Adrian. I start to head out the door to find a private place to watch them, but then I look back at Alia. Her face is buried in her pillow and she'd look almost lifeless if it weren't for the occasional twitch of her foot. I should try to talk to her. She's been really withdrawn since the other day, which I'm guessing is a result of her apparent fallout with Jaren.

"Alia," I begin, "I know we haven't talked very much lately, but I still consider you one of my closest friends, and if you — "

I'm cut off by a loud snore from Alia. Since my attempt at consoling her is futile, I leave the room and head to the recreation lounge, wondering at Alia's transformation. I almost liked her better when she was with Jaren all the time. I had considered telling her about almost being strangled in the hover chamber, but she generally hasn't been in a listening mood. Plus, I kind of just want to forget about the whole thing. I check a clock in the hallway. I only have about 30 minutes before lectures this afternoon.

The lounge is empty except for a few people messing around at the aerial obstacle course. I find a couch in the corner and apply the Adhesive from my mom onto my temple. Immediately I'm surrounded by the dusty recording room from my compound, with my mother and Daniel's faces in front of me. The room is dull and drab as usual, but for some reason it makes me homesick.

"Mari, we were so thrilled to finally hear from you!" My mother exclaims. She looks beautiful and confident as always, except for some faint lines at the corners of her mouth that make me wonder if her smile is as fake as mine was.

"Everything's been pretty normal here," she continues, *"except for a minor incident with the Restrainers."*

"Oh, man you should have s-s-seen it, Mari!" Daniel interrupts excitedly. *"They were running through a-all the fields at the farm, trampling d-d-d-down all the crops, and they were so fast! But they n-never found —"*

"It blew over in a week," my mother says quickly, *"it was just a misunderstanding."* She has a tone of strict finality in her voice. Daniel looks like he might have added something, but quickly shuts his mouth. I'm unaccustomed to seeing my mother so tense.

"Anyway," my mother says, forcing a smile, *"we really miss having you around here. It gets lonely with just the two of us."*

"Yeah," Daniel cuts in again, *"we spend m-m-most nights cleaning or doing puzzles or boring stuff l-like that."*

"It's not all bad," my mom counters, *"we still play plenty of games."*

"Yeah, but y-y-you always let me w-win. At least when M-Mari was here it was a challenge."

"Well, I guess I'll have to do something about that," my mom teases as she reaches over and squeezes Daniel's shoulder.

I sigh. I knew I missed my family, but I didn't realize just how much until now.

"Th-they switched out the holograph machine at s-s-s-school!" Daniel pipes up, shrugging off my mom's hand. *"Now the films look e-e-even more real and it projects all around us so it f-feels like w-we're in the movies! And we g-got new uniforms, and they t-took away the outdoor equipment a-a-and built big walls all around that are r-really fun to climb, even though we're not supposed to,"* he finishes in one breath.

"Yes, they've made a lot of changes at the school," my mother adds, furrowing her brow. There's that tense look again. *"But our time is almost up,"* she announces. *"We'd love to hear more about the friends you've made. Have you met any boys?"* She adds mischievously. Daniel makes a face that mirrors the way I feel. *"Anyway, we love you, honey,"* she looks straight into the camera, *"and I hope you're staying true to who you are."*

"Bye Mari!" Daniel shouts. The image dissolves slowly until I'm left staring at a wall in the recreation lounge.

I feel unsettled. It was wonderful to see my mom and brother, but something is definitely off back at our compound. What were the Restrainers looking for? And why were they at the farm of all places? I can't imagine

116

what they would have found threatening there. Maybe it's like my mother said, just a misunderstanding.

But what about building walls around the school? Almost sounds like they're making a prison. Which, incidentally, wouldn't be that far off the mark in my opinion.

I look around for a clock. I can't see any from where I'm sitting. I don't know how much time I have before our afternoon lecture. Maybe my Amplifier can find one.

"Mari, find out what time it is."

I expect for my body to go locate a clock, but instead my eyes quickly locate all the shadows in the room and my brain runs through various calculations until I hear myself say: "It is 4:17pm." I shake my head to rid myself of the invasive feeling of having my mind accessed by the Amplifier again. I should have worded the command more carefully. Next time I'll tell myself to go find a clock.

I sit back and stick Adrian's Adhesive onto my temple. Adrian's face appears in front of me. His bulk still surprises me. It looks like he's in an office at one of the factories.

"Hey sis! Are you loving being Amplified? Let me tell ya, it's totally worth it. Last week I was a bouncer for one of the clubs. I didn't mind that at all," he hints, grinning slyly. *Yeah, I'll bet,* I think. He probably had his pick of dopey, admiring girls. *"But this week I'm running the medical supplies factory! I'm in charge of so many people! It's incredible! There have been a couple of problems, but I can always work them out with the*

Amplifier." I bite the side of my mouth as I imagine Adrian fixing machinery or working out disagreements among the factory workers. How much is he letting his Amplifier do for him?

"So you're having trouble fitting in, huh?" He says with a smirk. *"I'm glad you came to your big brother for advice. Listen, I know what you're talking about. I felt the same way when I started Training. Let's face it, we were raised differently. Mom and dad taught us things in a way that don't really coincide with the Community's expectations. I mean, I know they meant well, what with the games and all, but they kind of put us at a disadvantage. Don't worry, though, you'll assimilate soon enough. Well, gotta get back to work. People need direction, and those supplies aren't going to assemble themselves!"* Adrian stands to leave and the office dissolves.

I lean forward and rub my temples. I think my jovial brother has just given me a headache. Assimilate? That sounds like a term straight from the Equality Movement. But maybe that's my problem. Why am I trying so hard to be different? Because I was raised contrary to the Community's guidelines? Did my parents do us a disservice by having us play those games?

I reflect on those evenings with my family. We always knew when it was time to play the games. Every night between 7 and 8 o' clock the steady whir of the cameras in our house would shut off. I don't know if the Community was trying to save energy or what, but regardless, we were left with an hour each evening with no threat of intrusion into our private lives.

It started out with stupid things Adrian and I did, like seeing who could make the other laugh first or who could hold their breath longer. Then my mother formalized our activities and we started having nightly competitions. The minute the cameras turned off we'd race to my mom to find out what she had planned. She'd place a Hydration capsule in front of us after we ran laps around the house and instruct us not to take it. Or we'd see who could stand on one foot or hold a rock in their outstretched hand the longest. One time she walked around the house and knocked things over or dropped things at random, and we'd jump up and try to be the first to find whatever is was to set it straight again. My mom had new games almost every night. They were all different, but most had a common theme: don't give in.

Sometimes my dad would come up with games too, but they'd usually involve helping one of the neighbors. Adrian hated when we did this, but I always thought it was kind of fun. Most nights near the end of that hour my parents would pray. I'd see them in their room, kneeling together and taking turns talking out loud. Sometimes I'd be confused at some of the things they said, but I never asked them about it. I didn't even know that what they were doing was called praying until Adrian explained it to me. Once I asked my mom who she and dad were talking to. She smiled, and after some hesitation, she said: "someone who cares."

After my father died, we stopped playing the games for a while. But my mother kept praying, all by herself. Some days she'd spend that whole hour when the cameras shut off praying in her room while I took care of Daniel. He was only 3 then. I remember hoping that the person she was talking to still cared.

A year later, when Adrain started his Service, my mother suddenly started the games again. It was almost comical to watch Daniel try to grasp the concepts. I felt bad competing against him, but soon enough he began to understand, and I often found myself struggling to beat a toddler. I guess, in a way, the games were how the three of us were able to cope with the loss of my father. They were a reminder that we are in charge of how we react to the tests life presents to us.

I jump up as I realize no one else is in the lounge anymore. I don't know how long I've been sitting here reminiscing about my family. I might already be late for the lecture. Hoping there's still time, I take a chance with my Amplifier.

"Mari, get into your seat in the lecture room by 4:30."

My body explodes into a run. I clear out of the recreation lounge in seconds and wince as I realize that I haven't been running in weeks. Once outside, my body goes into a series of gymnastic maneuvers, allowing me to cover the distance with flips and jumps much faster than I would have by merely running. I finish with an elaborate spin through the air as I reach the doors of the building. I sprint down the hall and catch a glimpse of a clock. I only have a few seconds.

The door to the lecture room is just starting to close as it comes into view. I dart through the opening. Almost everyone is already in their seats, meaning that I'll have to climb over quite a few people to get to my chair. However, the Amplifier apparently doesn't see this as a problem. I jump onto the table nearest me, startling the people who are sitting at it, and then leap animal-like from table to table until I land conspicuously in my seat next to Alia in the third row.

I wish I would have just chosen to be late.

Talina is fuming, and everyone is staring at me in disbelief. I feel my cheeks reddening. I look down and nervously rub the end of my shortened finger. I'm wishing I could just crawl under the table.

"Mari," Talina says coldly, "this isn't the Coliseum. There is no need for elaborate displays in the classroom."

"I'm sorry, I was just running late and I wanted to get here on time," I reply feebly.

"Well, I appreciate your commitment," she remarks, although she says it in a way that makes it clear that she does *not* appreciate my commitment. "Next time, try to keep in mind — "

She is cut short by someone bursting through the door. Everyone turns around in their seats to see the latecomer.

It's Liam, but it takes me a few seconds to recognize him.

"Wow," Alia whispers, "he looks good."

And he does look good. Apart from the fact that he looks like he's going to collapse, he's actually very attractive. His facial features are sharper and more handsome now that his chubby cheeks are gone, and he's wearing a smaller, tighter uniform that shows off his defined upper body and newly flattened stomach. It really is impressive. And a little unnerving.

There are gasps and whispers from around the room. I look back at Talina, wondering how she's going to react. To my surprise, she's smiling.

"Liam, go get some sleep," she tells him, "you deserve it."

For a minute, it seems like Liam might just stay because he's enjoying all the attention of his peers. But after a moment, he concedes.

"Ok, thanks," he says simply as he turns to leave. It might be my imagination, but I'm pretty sure he flexed his buttocks before walking out.

"All right, everyone," Talina announces, still smiling a little, "let's talk about how to diffuse explosives."

Everyone's looking at Talina, but it's obvious that we're all still a little distracted. For my part, I'm just grateful that Liam's transformation was shocking enough to make everyone forget about my extravagant entrance.

Chapter 18

I wince as I watch Cassidy make contact with the live cables a second time. She screams and starts flailing around, apparently losing all resolve to free herself. After a few seconds, Justin shuts off the power to the room and Cassidy goes limp, hanging over a low cable.

We've finally found out the purpose of the electrocution-jungle room: to test our agility and flexibility by maneuvering through the cables without getting shocked. When we reach the other side of the room, we're supposed to press a button that retracts the cables so we can easily cross back to the entrance. Justin, in his overbearing way, has been monitoring our progress. Although, I can't say his help is unwelcome. No one wants to be stuck in dozens of jolt-infused cables, and so far, not one of us has made it to the button.

Cassidy groans and half-falls off the cable, looking drained as she limps back to the group. She stands behind me and says, "At first I kinda liked the shocks, but then they just started wiping me out." I give her an odd look and she shrugs her shoulders.

"You guys have got to think harder!" Justin growls, turning the power back on and reigniting the electricity of the dangerous cables. "You have unlimited possibilities with your Amplifiers, use them! You're all being too narrow-minded!"

"Will you give us a hint?" Someone asks from the back of the group.

"No!" Justin spits. "That's the problem! You're used to being given everything! You've got to think for yourselves!"

We all fall silent. So far, we've watched dozens of trainees climb walls, do intricate acrobatics, shimmy across the floor, and execute massive feats of strength in an attempt to get past the cables, all to no avail. I'm starting to wonder what kind of mental creativity is needed to overcome this course. Suddenly, a girl near me breaks the silence.

"But, aren't inventive ideas contrary to the Equality Movement?" She ventures. "I mean, if it's really important, then we can just rely on the Override, right?" Justin stares at her blankly, then exhales deeply, shakes his head, and walks away.

We all look around at each other awkwardly, I guess searching for a clue as to what to do next. Eventually, the group starts to disperse, wandering off to various other parts of the Coliseum. I linger behind, studying the cable jungle and thinking about what that girl said. She did have a point; the Equality Movement does discourage extraordinary behavior and we've been conditioned to receive answers and special skills just for the asking. So why would anyone go to any length to excel or succeed?

I glance around. Everyone from the group has left and the people closest to me are busy watching two people fighting in the pool. I peer through the cables again, trying to see a path to the button on the wall, but every clear route ends in an almost solid tangle of cables.

I walk forward almost involuntarily, knowing with every step that I'm probably making a huge mistake. *Am I really going to try to get through this room without someone here to shut off the power?*

I look at the angles of the cables, trying to figure out how I'm going to have to contort my body to get through them. I remember watching an old movie on our holograph machine about a school group that competed in a unique type of dance. What was it called again? After a moment I remember.

"Mari, break dance through the cables to get to the button."

I drop to the floor and my body wriggles in a wavelike motion underneath the first two cables. My legs kick up and suddenly I'm upright again, clearing several more cables by hopping from one foot to the other. I bend backwards and slide underneath a particularly low-hanging wire, then plant my hands on the floor behind me and spin my body past a group of tightly clumped cords. I jump in between a set of low and high cables, noticing that they sway dangerously close to my head when I pass through. I do a flip off of one hand, and land directly on top of one of the cables.

The shocks course through my body. It's not strong enough to knock me out, but it hurts like crazy and makes it hard to think straight. I fall to the floor, thankfully in a spot clear of the cables, but I'm in the middle of the room and my body is still attempting to dance. I kick up again and go into a spinning flip, rotating one and a half times and landing in a low handstand. My legs lower to pass through a couple wires, but don't get low enough and instead get twisted up in them.

I cry out as my body starts convulsing, a combination of the electrocution of the cables and my body still trying to complete the command. I'm hanging upside down, becoming more tangled in the wires with every move I make, like a fly caught in a spider web. I'm in agony, and the repeated jolts from the wires are starting to burn through the pants of my uniform. I'm beginning to lose consciousness when suddenly the electric shocks cease.

I let myself hang there for a moment, trying to get up the energy to detach myself from the cords. I crane my neck to look behind me and see that someone is standing by the power switch. The person walks toward me and soon I can see that it's Liam.

"You really like to get yourself into dangerous situations, don't you?" Liam comments, with just a slight hint of mockery in his voice. I barely have the energy to respond.

"Help," I croak. My throat is dry. I must have been yelling more than I realized. Liam gingerly pulls my feet out of the cables and sets them on the floor.

"Looks like you'll need a new uniform," Liam says, eyeing the burnt holes in my pant legs.

"Yeah," I say weakly, "maybe I can have your old one."

Liam snickers. "Sure, if you want to wear a tent."

I look up at him. It's still weird to see him all toned and trim. I slowly get to my feet.

"How is it that you're always the one to come to my rescue?" I ask him.

"Maybe I'm your guardian angel," he jokes, winking. "Plus, you're someone I don't want to lose," he adds more seriously. I smile, but I don't really know what to make of that comment. He's saved me twice now, but that could just be a coincidence. Maybe he's just observant and happens to help a lot of people out. In any case, I want to change the subject.

"I don't know how anyone can get through this room, it's crazy!"

"Yeah," Liam agrees, "I haven't seen anyone make it yet. I think you have to give yourself multiple commands while you're going through it, just one command for the whole course doesn't cut it."

I nod my head, recalling how the break dancing worked at first, but then the moves stopped lining up with the clear spaces.

"But the patterns switch so fast, you'd have to be a genius to pull that off," I retort in exasperation.

"Or a Miles Paxton."

I hesitate. Maybe the shocks messed with my brain. *Did Liam just say what I think he did?*

"A what?"

"Oh, it's something we say in my compound," Liam responds. "When someone does something that seems impossible, we call it a Miles Paxton."

"Did you know him?" I ask tentatively.

127

"Of course not! It's just a made up story about someone who broke into our control tower. He doesn't actually exist."

"Oh, I see," I remark quietly. But now my already aching brain is throbbing with this new piece of information. Did Miles wreak havoc in other compounds, or is this just a rumor that got passed to other people and was altered in the process? How many other compounds talk about Miles Paxton? Is he some kind of legend for the whole Community?

"Mari, are you okay?" Liam asks, bringing me back to reality. I don't know how long I've been standing here musing about Miles, but I'm sure I have a really ridiculous look on my face.

"I don't know," I hedge, "I think those electrocution cables really did a number on me. I'm going to go back to my dorm to lie down."

"Ok, let me know if you need anything," Liam offers.

"I will," I tell him. "And Liam, thank you. I really owe you one."

"You owe me two," he teases, winking at me again.

I walk back to my dorm thinking mostly about Miles, but once or twice about the odd sensation I feel when Liam winks at me.

Chapter 19

"Hey, do you know what Talina just said about our assessment? I missed it," I whisper to Alia.

"I don't know," she responds blandly, "and I really don't care." I try to hide my frustration at her apathy, but there's no need. Alia might as well be dead to the world. For the past few weeks she's been barely more than merely existing, and I'm afraid she's not going to pass the final exam. I mean, I understand that break ups can be hard, at least from what I've seen in movies and the stories my mom used to tell me about her younger days, but this seems a little extreme. And lately every time I try to talk to her about it, she either erupts into a yelling fit or leaves the room. Or both.

"She said we'd need to be successful with at least 80 percent of the weapons in order to pass," Joby whispers to me.

"Thanks, Joby," I say flatly. He looks really pleased with himself. I can't bring myself to tell him that I already knew what Talina said and was just trying to get Alia to listen. Joby has started sitting next to me during lectures now. I guess he's not really friends with Liam anymore.

We're listening to Talina tell us all the most important things to remember for our assessment, which is only two weeks away. If Alia doesn't pull herself together, she'll have her Amplifier removed and end up doing labor for the rest of her life, most likely back at the farm she hates so much. Could this idiot Jaren have messed her up so much that she no longer cares about her future?

"You will be observed by four Restrainers who will report back to Governor Plenaris," Talina states. Her mention of the Governor makes the room erupt in excited whispers. I don't know why everyone's so thrilled about this, I can't imagine the Restrainers relaying anything more than whether we pass or fail to Governor Plenaris. Unless, of course, someone were to mess up so badly that they set themselves apart. Personally, I'm more interested in the Restrainers being present at our assessment. Adrian told me a couple stories about watching them in action. Their special Amplification allows them to process and perform better than everyone else. Maybe we'll get to witness their enhanced abilities while they're here.

"Basically, you'll be just fine if you follow the rules and don't say the wrong thing," Talina finishes with a grim smile. From the front row, Tristan raises his hand.

"What if we do say the wrong thing?" He asks. "I mean, what if we accidentally give ourselves the wrong command? Can we give ourselves another command to stop it?"

Usually I expect everything that comes out of Tristan's mouth will be stupid or irrelevant, but I'm actually interested to know the answer to his question.

"No, you cannot stop it," Talina responds dryly. "You can only give yourself another command once the previous one has been completed or becomes impossible to perform."

"So there's no way to resist it?" Tristan says timidly.

"No Amplified person has ever been able to stop themselves from carrying out a command," Talina replies. She studies Tristan for a moment and adds, "If it is a serious matter than it can be resolved in an Override."

Tristan looks relieved, but doesn't say anything else. I wonder what serious mistake he made. But what bothers me even more is the fact that it's impossible to resist an Amplifier. Is there really no one with the will power strong enough to combat a command?

"This concludes your formal training," Talina announces, regaining everyone's attention. "For the next two weeks you will each be responsible for practicing and reviewing skills on your own. Justin and I will be available to offer assistance if absolutely necessary, but please don't come to us with frivolous questions as we will be busy setting up for the assessment." She turns off the screen and reaches down to pick up the silver Override box, then turns back to face us. "Good luck."

———-

"What do you think Tristan commanded himself to do that needs to be fixed?" Joby muses, craning his neck to look at Tristan across the nutrition hall. He and Cassidy are intent on a piece of paper on the table in front of them, whispering back and forth and looking anxious.

"Why don't you go ask him?" I respond, popping a Satisfy capsule into my mouth. I know I'm being rude, but I'm getting sick of Joby trying to engage me in conversation. Actually, I'm just getting sick of Joby, he's been following me around relentlessly for weeks.

"Nah, it's probably something stupid, anyway," Joby concedes, confirming my suspicion that he really didn't care much in the first place. "So what do you think you're gonna do for the next two weeks?" He asks.

"Practice and review," I say curtly.

"I think I'm going to take it easy for a little while," Joby volunteers, despite my not having asked him. "You know, rest up so I'm not so stressed for the assessment." He stretches his arms above his head as if demonstrating that he's ready to start relaxing right now. I study him for a moment. I hadn't realized how muscular his arms had become, and I can see that his pectorals are much more defined. He looks healthier in general, probably a result of being able to sleep more regularly. I guess all the trainees have improved their physique in one way or another. Well, except for Alia, who has inexplicably gained weight. I watch her sullenly poke at her bowl of capsules, then pick out a Pleasure. She raises it to her mouth and then says:

"Alia, don't eat it."

Her hand automatically drops the capsule and she goes back to poking at her bowl. Her command to avoid the Pleasure capsule makes me think of Liam, who said he'd commanded himself to hate them. I scan the room until I see him. We make eye contact and he waves at me. I smile and wave back.

"Hey Mari," Joby says quickly, "do you want me to get you some more capsules?"

I sigh. "Sure, Joby."

He leaves the table and goes over to the dispensers. I know full well why he wanted my attention right then, but I still don't like to think about it. Instead I let my thoughts drift back to Liam, about his dramatic physical change that cost him some of his personality. Will his command to hate Pleasure capsules stay in effect forever? What other aspects of someone's personality is the Amplifier capable of changing?

I start observing the people around me and listen to some of the things they're commanding themselves to do.

"Devon, go talk to that girl."

"Ronda, don't eat anymore right now."

"Brady, calm down."

"Calvin, remember to lift weights tonight."

"Charlotte, don't stare at him."

"Jack, tell a funny joke."

"Morgan, throw this trash away."

The more I listen, the more horrified I become. We're using our Amplifiers to do the simple, mundane tasks we used to be able to do ourselves. Have we become so dependent that we can no longer think, act, or feel without the aid of the device implanted in our heads?

"I got a couple of every capsule because I wasn't sure which ones you like," Joby announces, interrupting my thoughts. He plops a bowl in front of me. I fish out a Hydration and swallow it quickly.

"Thanks Joby," I say, "but I'm not feeling very good, I'm going to take a walk."

"Hey, I'll come with you," he offers.

"No!" I respond, a little more harshly than I intended. "I mean, I just... I'd really like to be alone right now."

I turn away and walk out of the nutrition hall as fast as I can.

Chapter 20

I reposition my pillow for the tenth time tonight. It seems like I've been staring into the dark for hours — sleep just will not come. And Alia's not even crying, which is usually what keeps me awake. Every time I start to drift off, Talina's words about not being able to resist the Amplifier run through my head and jar me back to consciousness. I don't know why it bothers me so much. I mean, if people were able to withstand their Amplifiers, they wouldn't be as effective. But it's just hard to believe that, "no Amplified person has ever been able to stop themselves from carrying out a command."

I get out of bed. Clearly I won't be falling asleep anytime soon, so there's no use just lying there staring at the ceiling. A plan starts forming in my head. I'm careful not to wake anyone as I put on my shoes and slip out the door.

It's a clear, cool night. I look up at the stars as I walk across the deck of the barge. They're shining so brightly that I don't have any problem seeing where I'm going. As far as I can recall, there are no cameras outside of the recording room, but I still walk around and double check when I get there. I end up on the side facing the edge of the barge, where the building hides me from view and there's about 12 feet of deck before it drops off into the darkness.

I take a deep breath. I am fairly positive that this is a stupid idea. But I just want to know how hard it really is to resist the Amplifier.

"Mari, do a back flip."

Before I have time to even think, my body squats down and propels itself backward, performing a flawless back flip. I shake out my arms and legs and close my eyes, trying to concentrate on keeping my feet planted on the ground this time before giving myself the command.

"Mari, do a back flip."

There's a slight pain in my legs as I fight to keep them in place, but other than that, nothing keeps my body from completing the back flip. *Looks like this is going to be harder than I thought*, I think. I center myself again and try a new tactic.

I think about my father. When he worked on his carvings, he would be so focused that nothing could distract him. He wouldn't stop until his wood carving was perfect. Sometimes you'd speak to him for several minutes before he'd notice that you were trying to talk to him. I really miss watching him carve out those elaborate designs. He was so methodical and exact. If I could just channel that kind of focus, maybe I could overcome these commands.

I fill my mind with thoughts of my father as I give myself the command to do a back flip again. My body tenses as I work hard against the mechanical movements being forced by the Amplifier. I'm slower to comply this time, and as a result, I falter halfway through the flip and land on my stomach instead of my feet. It's progress, at least, even though I got the wind knocked out of me.

I roll over onto my back and give the command again. I try to keep myself lying on the ground for as long as possible, but it's only a few seconds before I feel myself stand up and go through the motions. I command myself to do the back flip about a dozen times in succession, thinking maybe if I wear my body out it will make it weaker than my will power, but it seems to have the opposite effect.

I command myself while clinging to the side of the building, feeling my finger pads burn as I try to hold on to the brick walls. I command myself starting from several different positions, and while I'm able to hinder The Amplifier a little bit, every time I more or less complete the back flip, but not without incurring a collection of scratches and bruises. I'm completely exhausted and I know that I should give up and go back to bed, but I know by now that I wasn't raised to give up.

I shake myself off and walk to the very edge of the barge. A part of me can't believe I'm about to try this, but I'm so determined to overcome the Amplifier that I'm driven to extremes. *Surely I won't comply with the command if it's a matter of life or death, right?*

A gust of wind rushes past me as I look over the side of the barge. I can't see how high up we are, but I know that if I do a back flip from here I will be falling to my death. *What are you doing, Mari? Is it really worth it?* Of course it isn't, but I also know this is the only way to really motivate myself to go against the Amplifier.

I turn around so that my back is to the edge. I stand there for a few minutes, trying to calm my nerves and psyching myself up for what I'm about to do. Finally, I close my eyes and slowly give myself the command one more time.

"Mari, do a back flip."

I feel my legs start to jerk upwards but strain as hard as I can against the automatic urge. My whole body is shaking and I stumble back a couple inches, causing one of my feet to momentarily dangle off the side. I start to panic. I didn't think this through. Did I think the Amplifier would just stop after a few seconds of noncompliance? Talina said the command would remain in effect until completed. I can't hold off these powerful impulses forever.

My body aches and my head is throbbing. I feel convulsions in my stomach as the Amplifier tries to force me backwards. I think about how good it would feel to just yield to the sensations coursing through my body, but in the next moment remember that to comply would mean certain death. My endurance is almost spent and I'm getting weaker, but I just hold on to the fact that I desperately want to live. In an effort to motivate myself, I open my mouth and scream at the top of my lungs:

"DON'T GIVE IN!"

The words echo across the barge and come back to me. Slowly, I feel the robotic compulsions of the Amplifier subside, and I don't have to fight anymore. I exhale and take a few shaky steps away from the edge, repeating over and over, "That was so stupid, that was so stupid..." But somewhere beneath all my fatigue is a feeling of triumph. *I did it, I overcame the amplifier.* I turn back to face the edge that a few minutes ago I was struggling so vehemently against. In my relieved delirium, I start to laugh.

Then suddenly my body tenses up and does a back flip.

Chapter 21

"What happened to you?"

"Personal experiment," I grumble in response to Joby's worried inquiry. I have scratches all over my face and a huge bruise on my arm. I suppose that I should be proud that I held off the Amplifier for so long last night, but I'm still frustrated that it got me in the end, almost like it was having the last laugh.

"Are you going to make a habit of these ... uh, personal experiments?" Joby presses.

"I don't think so," I reply, rubbing a sore spot on my hip.

"Good," Joby says and pops some Protein capsules into his mouth. I bite back a nasty remark. It's nice that he cares about me, but it's not like I need to be taken care of.

"Have you seen Alia?" I ask instead.

"Yeah, she's over there with Jaren," Joby answers, pointing across the nutrition hall. I see Alia standing at a table talking with Jaren. For a minute I'm hopeful that they're making up, but after watching them for a while it's clear that they're in a heated argument. I'm too far away from them to hear what they're saying, but I can tell that Alia is far more angry than Jaren. She keeps throwing her hands in the air while he stands with his arms folded across his chest looking only slightly perturbed. Finally, Jaren spreads his hands as if to say, *"What do you want me to do about it?"* and Alia stomps away, probably to go lay in her bed for the next several hours. I let out an involuntary growl.

"What was that for?" Joby says, looking around at me quizzically.

"Oh, it's nothing, really," I respond. "I just wish Alia would get over this funk already."

Joby raises his eyebrows at me, frowning a bit. Is there something he knows that I don't?

There isn't time to find out. Suddenly, there is frantic screaming coming from outside on the deck. I'm not sure if we're all driven by curiosity or fear, but everyone runs out of the nutrition hall to see what's going on. When I get outside, my heart jumps into my throat.

The sky is filled with a dozen massive air ships. They're like nothing I've ever seen before; sleek, black, oval-shaped carriers hovering over the barge and systematically firing down on all of us helpless victims below. I see a few people staggering around with bleeding arms or legs, but so far, it seems no one is mortally wounded. Yet. A group of trainees run back into the nutrition hall, but it seems their movement does not go unnoticed. A moment later several explosions rip the nutrition hall apart. Apparently, nowhere is safe.

What is happening? I feel like I'm frozen in place while people are running frantically across the deck of the barge, with no direction, no plan. It reminds me of when I first watched those water droplets float around in the hover chamber. Here we all are, with infinite potential, and no power. We might as well not be Amplified.

And then I have a fleeting memory of the architecture of the air barge, something I saw in school. While the shots and explosions are demolishing the buildings, the deck of the barge seems to suffer no damage. We need to get under the deck.

"Mari, recall the layout of the air barge."

Immediately my mind fills with diagrams and designs. I glance around and can imagine the structural organization of the barge, its technology and architecture. I look down and see the fissures in the floor, and with the aid of my Amplifier, recollect that they open up into large compartments. I further recall that the deck panels are controlled by a lever on the Northwest corner of the barge.

A bullet flies by my face and incites me to action. I run toward the site where I just pictured the lever, dodging bullets and screaming trainees on my way there. I have to jump over a few people lying on the ground, either too injured or too stunned to move. A building explodes to the right of me, and I'm knocked to the ground by a chunk of cement that hits me in the shoulder. I know I'm bleeding badly and likely have one or more broken bones, but I'm determined to follow through with my plan.

"Mari, keep running to the lever."

My body fights through the pain and I'm up and going again. Finally, I see the small building that houses the controls. There is an electronic lock on the door. I'm not keen on giving my Amplifier complete control again, but I feel like this is an emergency.

"Mari, find out the passcode."

I vaguely recognize my brain going through thousands of algorithms and probabilities, along with an analysis of the wear on various numbers on the lock. Within seconds, my fingers are punching in the code: 479902. The doors spring open and I rush inside. There are a number of other controls and monitoring screens along the walls, but I go straight to a large lever at the back of the room and pull it down. On some of the screens I see the various panels of the deck are opening up, sliding apart to reveal the compartments below. I run back outside.

"Everybody get yourselves and everyone around you into the compartments!" I'm screaming at every person I pass, careful to avoid the panels that are open. Some people have already fallen into the holes, some immediately obey, and some stare at me in bewilderment so I have to point animatedly at the openings until they catch on.

One girl gives me trouble.

"Why would we want to get in those? Won't it just be easier for them to shoot at us if we have nowhere to go?"

She does have a point. That's why we need to hurry so I can close the panels again. Luckily, the concept seems to be catching on. I look down the expanse of the deck and see that almost everyone has escaped into one of the compartments. I run back to the small building and pull the lever back up. On the screens I can see the panels closing slowly. Painstakingly slow.

But eventually all the compartments are sealed again and everyone is safe. Everyone except for me.

As if validating my thoughts, the roof on the building I'm in suddenly explodes. Through falling debris, I glance up and see a ship hovering over my location, its guns repositioning themselves to find me. I scramble out of the damaged building and start running toward the edge of the barge. I can hear the bullets ricocheting off the floor of the deck behind me, perhaps some of them even hit me, but I'm so full of adrenaline that I don't feel them. I'm about 20 feet away from a free fall and I've got to decide on a plan of action.

"Mari, flip over the edge and grab hold of the underside of the barge."

I don't even think I know what that means, but I'm hoping the Amplifier will pull through. I reach the end of the deck and my body twists into a sharp back flip off the edge, ironically the very move I was fighting against the night before. My back arches enough to let my hands connect with the bottom of the barge, and the next moment I'm inexplicably grasping on to two of the many small crevices on the vessel's underbelly. The rest of my body swings around and slams into the barge, testing the limits of my already precarious hand holds.

There's a set of protruding bars about 10 feet in, and my body works its way slowly over to them, my hands maneuvering expertly along a dozen almost imperceptible cracks until they're able to get a firm and lasting grip on the bars. I know my fingers are going to ache later, but for now, I just hang underneath the barge until the terrifying sounds of the sleek air ships fade away.

————-

The face of the air barge looks like something from the ancient war films they would show us in school. About one-third of the buildings are destroyed, some still smoking from the explosions. When I finally climbed back on deck, I saw that everyone was already out of the compartments. Apparently Justin pulled the lever to open up all the floor panels. I wonder where he and Talina were during this disaster. It looks like most of the trainees have come back to their senses. Roughly half of them are using their Amplifiers to treat their own and others people's injuries. When I walk by, trainees are either staring at me in awe or giving me small, grateful smiles. Altogether I feel really awkward.

"Mari! I'm so glad you're okay!" Joby shouts as he comes running up to me. I realize that I'm glad he's okay too. "I was so worried about you! Where did you go?" He continues, wrapping his arms around me. I return his hug hesitantly as I answer his question.

"I went underneath the barge. Luckily there was something under there to hold on to."

"You're amazing, Mari."

"Thanks, Joby. I appreciate that." And I do. I know any moment I'm going to get a lecture from Talina or Justin about my rash behavior, so I decide to take as much praise for my actions as I can get right now. I gently shrug out of Joby's embrace in time to see Alia running into our dorm, which was thankfully spared from the destruction. When I look back at Joby, he's frowning at something behind me.

"Hey Mari, you got a hero complex or something?" I turn around to see Liam approaching. He's grinning, but I can tell that underneath he's a little shaken - he's more jittery than usual.

"Either that or a suicide complex," I respond, a little more seriously than I would have liked.

"Well, that was pretty awesome what you did back there," Liam admits. "I don't know if anyone else here would have had the presence of mind to pull that off." Out of the corner of my eye I see that Joby has stomped off. But before I can counter Liam's comment, I hear the voice I've been expecting to hear since I climbed back up on deck.

"Mari, I need you to come with me." Talina's voice punctures the small amount of self-assurance I had built up. I turn to face her, but to my surprise, she doesn't look upset. She looks drained.

"Follow me."

She leads me back to the control room where I went the first day of training to defend my actions of saving Tristan. I wonder how I'm going to defend myself against this. A part of me doesn't even want to. We descend the stairs to the small, dark room where I'm met with the unwelcome sight of Governor Plenaris.

146

Chapter 22

"Miss Quillen, have a seat," the Governor says smoothly, as if we were sitting down for a friendly chat. He looks severely out of place with his gray suit and calm expression. Sometimes I wonder if his face is made out of plastic.

"Miss Quillen, I have been monitoring your behavior these past few months, and it seems you have only increased your efforts to set yourself apart from the others, this recent instance being the most grievous of your actions." I feel an exclamation of defense rising up in my throat, but I silence it. "Talina has been sending me written reports, but I've found the video footage of your conduct to be much more illuminating. Let's review it, shall we?"

He presses a button on the wall and several screens light up, showing me in the Coliseum attacking the manikin by combining the bow staff skills with acrobatics. Next, I watch myself heal my ankle in minutes, with Talina looking on. I wince as I relive that episode, remembering the intense pain that made me wish I was dead. Next, the screens show me in the hover chamber, defeating the three other trainees by ultimately shutting off the anti-gravity switch. I gasp as I suddenly recall what happened just after that event, and before I can stop myself, I speak up.

"Do you happen to have the footage from a few minutes after - ?"

"I will let you know when you are permitted to ask questions," Governor Plenaris cuts in sharply. I close my mouth and stare at my hands. I rub the stunted end of my seared-off finger, trying to get my anger to subside. I wonder what would happen if I stood up and attacked the Governor right now. Would all my other finger tips be burned off on contact? I wonder if he has as many security measures surrounding his actual body as he does his hologram. Probably. Probably more.

I look up in time to see the end of my over-the-top entrance into the lecture room last week. It's almost comical watching the reactions of the other trainees, I guess I really surprised some of them. Finally the view switches to today's disaster. The terror returns as I watch people being shot at and buildings exploding. I can see now that a few trainees were attempting to use their Amplifiers against the attacks, but their actions were largely ineffective. I don't care to watch myself dodge bullets and open up the panels. It's fresh in my mind, there's no need to review. Instead, I feel myself growing more and more indignant. *What is the Governor playing at?* People have been injured and buildings have been destroyed and he's choosing to review all of my stunts? Shouldn't he be addressing this unprecedented attack? Doesn't he have more pressing concerns than watching videos of an insignificant girl make innocent mistakes? Just how much of a threat am I?

I snap out of my thoughts when I realize that the video has ended and the Governor is addressing me again.

"Obviously, you have a habit of stepping out of line and using your skills in reckless and irresponsible ways. This footage displays an instability that, if left unchecked, can be hugely detrimental to the Amplification process, and that doesn't even include your direct attempt to overcome your Amplifier last night."

The shock on my face must be evident, because the Governor pauses momentarily, then adds:

"You were smart to find an area of the barge that is not covered by our cameras, but every command you give your Amplifier is tracked and the time of its completion recorded. Therefore, we saw that you commanded yourself to do a back-flip almost 40 times, and the speed with which your body responded on each one. On the last, you held off for almost 2 minutes, which is the longest anyone has ever resisted their Amplifier."

I stare at Governor Plenaris. He's stated it so indifferently, as if it were to be expected, but the fact that every Amplified act is documented makes me shutter.

"You needn't be shocked, Marianna," Governor Plenaris explains, "it's simply a safety precaution."

More like a sick way to be inside everybody's heads, I think.

"In any case, I think you need to reevaluate the way you have approached your Amplification," he continues, "particularly instances in which you have violated the Equality Movement..."

I can't take it anymore. The rage I feel toward this man is suddenly so acute that I abandon all civility and explode.

"If there are lives at stake and there's something I can do about it, I will not stand idly by for the sake of equality!" I yell at him. The Governor is silent, so I continue. "What just happened out there? Where did those ships come from and why were they trying to kill us? Why are you wasting time with me down here when something catastrophic has just happened up there?"

Talena looks shocked at my outburst, but Governor Plenaris' expression, as always, is unchanged. He takes a step forward and clears his throat.

"What you just witnessed was merely a simulation," he states, "a test of the effectiveness of your training."

I picture the demolished buildings and all those trainees stumbling around, wounded and bloody. I simply cannot believe it was a simulation. I look over at Talina for confirmation. At first she looks bewildered, but a moment later her face smooths over.

"That is correct," she says automatically. "In every Training cycle there is at least one instance of violent simulation to mimic real life experience. In the event that the simulation becomes truly dangerous, we institute the Override."

When she finishes speaking, she blinks several times and then looks almost angry, but she doesn't say any more. I catch the slightest movement of the Governor pressing something on his wrist. I'm more alarmed at this exchange than by anything else that's occurred in this meeting. I don't know how he did it, but I'm pretty sure Governor Plenaris forced her to say those words.

"So you see, Marianna, that your performance today was unwarranted and unnecessary," the Governor remarks with a note of finality. "The Restrainers will review your case and we will come to a decision concerning your future in the next few weeks. Until that time, Miss Quillen, you will continue with your training as normal, and I advise you to correct your irrational tendencies. You are dismissed."

——————-

It's dark when I come out of the control room, I must have been in there for hours. I'm seething from the whole exchange. I guess I knew from the first time I met with the Governor that I wasn't really going to change, but listening to his idiotic accusations just makes my blood boil. And to think at one point I revered the man.

He can lie all he wants to about what happened this afternoon, but I don't buy it for a minute. I know it wasn't a simulation, so I don't regret my "irrational tendencies" one bit. But now I'm consumed with who it was that attacked us and why Governor Plenaris is covering it up. What is he hiding?

And then there's the looming prospect of my life being decided by the Restrainers. It seemed like Governor Plenaris had already made up his mind about me, and I'm sure my emotional explosion just now didn't help much, so why prolong the inevitable? I suppose they have to take it to the Restrainers so that it satisfies the Equality Movement. I'm nearly ready to be done with it all anyway, with all the protocols and the limitations and the unnecessary invasions of privacy. If only I didn't enjoy being Amplified so much. Isn't there a way to keep my Amplifier and still make my own decisions? To not have my every move monitored?

Of course, there is the possibility that they'll decide to go beyond just the removal of my Amplifier. I've heard of the prisons, but I can't imagine that my actions would be considered criminal. Then again, I never imagined that the Governor of our entire Community would spend so much time worrying about a nobody like me. Great, now I'm going to have nightmares about being imprisoned.

When I walk into my dorm room, I hear that Alia is crying again. I'm about to tell her off, tell her that her problems are probably minuscule in comparison to mine, but then I realize that this is much different from her normal crying. She's sobbing. It's a heart-wrenching, gasping-for-breath kind of weeping, the kind you hear from someone who is utterly broken, the kind you don't interrupt. As my eyes adjust to the dark, I see the other girls are only pretending not to hear her. I catch Janet's eye, she shrugs and gives me a hopeless look.

I tip toe over to my bed and quietly lie down, resolving that I will find out what's wrong with Alia in the morning. I still have thoughts of Governor Plenaris and prison in the back of my mind, but they're overshadowed by my worries of what could possibly be ailing my friend. Somehow, I'm able to fall asleep while listening to Alia whisper, "I'm sorry, I'm so sorry," over and over again.

Chapter 23

"That was some kind of crazy simulation the other day, right?" Derek comments, almost dropping his hammer again.

"I know!" Hannah exclaims. "If they hadn't told us otherwise, I would still think it was a real attack."

"That's because they were *real* bullets and *real* explosions and they did *real* damage, which suspiciously doesn't happen in a simulation," I retort. I adjust the board I'm propping up with my shoulder and try to ignore the strange looks everyone is giving me. I should probably give up on trying to convince people that the attack wasn't just an elaborate training exercise. Why would they believe me anyway after they heard the explanation coming from Governor Plenaris himself?

The morning after the attack, they gathered all of us together and the Governor personally addressed us, spouting off the same crap about how the incident was actually a simulation, and how for the most part, we had failed. Everyone was so thrilled to be seeing Governor Plenaris in person that they didn't seem to mind that our punishment for "failing" was to reconstruct all the damaged buildings. So Talina and Justin divided us up into our animal tagging groups and for the past few days we've been rotating between building the destroyed structures and trying to train for our final assessment. Needless to say, tensions have been a little high.

Currently, we're working on putting one of the boy's dorms back together; its south-facing wall was blown off in one of the explosions. The dorm is still being used, despite the damage, and we can see into one of the rooms.

"Hey, whose bed is that with all the crumpled papers on it?" Todd asks.

"Ah, that's Tristan's bed," Liam answers, "he's always drawing stuff and throwing it away."

"That's weird," Hannah comments. "What's he drawing?"

"I don't know, looks like diagrams or something most of the time," Liam shouts over the sound of his drill.

"What's he trying to do? Escape from training?" Joby jokes. Everyone laughs and I laugh weakly along with them, but I'm afraid Tristan might actually be planning something far more catastrophic. I'm still wondering what it was that he accidentally commanded himself to do.

"Hey, is it okay if I work with you guys? My group is a little too much for me to handle right now."

We all look up from our work and see that Alia is standing behind us.

"We'll always welcome more help, just as long as your group is all right with it," Liam offers.

"I think they'll manage," Alia replies as she glances back at the recreation lounge. I can just barely make out the form of Jaren. It looks like he's giving orders while everyone else is hard at work. I don't blame Alia for leaving, Jaren's a jerk all on his own, even without whatever fallout the two of them had.

Alia immediately bends down and starts reinforcing some of the supports. I'm amazed at the way she's changed over these past few days. She's definitely not back to her old self; there's a profound sadness about her, but she seems stronger somehow and more determined to take charge of her life. I never did ask her what was wrong the other night, even though I promised myself I would. I guess I'm afraid that if I bring it up, she'll relapse into the empty listlessness that has conquered her life for the past several weeks.

After a couple hours, we hear the alarm that tells us it's time to go back to training. We definitely made some progress on the dorm. The wall is about halfway finished.

"Hey Mari, you want to come check out the urban obstacle course with me?" Joby asks.

Before I can say anything, Liam jumps in. "Actually, Mari, I was thinking you might want some help with the electrocution room."

I look back and forth between the two of them, not sure how to respond. Alia comes to my rescue.

"Mari and I are actually going to shower real quick before we start any training, we don't want to get dust all over the equipment."

"Oh, sure, good idea," Joby says quickly and turns to leave. Liam raises an eyebrow at me before following Joby to the Coliseum.

"Thanks for that," I say gratefully to Alia.

"Sure, that's what friends are for," she replies.

I feel a stab of guilt at the word "friends."

"Hey Alia, the other night..."

"Don't ask," Alia cuts in.

I let out a small laugh, wondering if she's joking. Although I guess this isn't something you would joke about. "What?"

"Don't ask," she repeats. "You don't want to know and I don't want to tell, so it's better to leave it alone."

I'm shocked at this response. I know it must have been an awful thing she went through, but I've never known Alia to turn down an opportunity to divulge the personal details of her life. She really has changed. She must sense the awkwardness, because suddenly she forces an excited tone and asks, "So who do you like more, Liam or Joby?"

This sudden mood change confuses me even more.

"I - I don't know," I say, glancing back toward the Coliseum where Liam and Joby just went. But what catches my eye is a small, curly haired boy sneaking into the nutrition hall.

"Felix," I say under my breath.

"Who's Felix?" Alia remarks with some interest.

"Uh, no one," I hedge. "I think I forgot something back there, I'll meet you in the Coliseum."

"Okay, see you later," Alia concedes. I know she's probably suspicious, but she doesn't press the matter.

I head to the nutrition hall at a brisk walk. I don't want to draw attention to myself, but I'm hoping I can catch Felix before he disappears this time. I'm thinking there's a possibility he might know something about the attack the other day, and I still want to know about the voice on the recording from my device.

The hall is empty, mostly everyone is probably in the Coliseum right now. There are still several gaping holes in the ceiling from the explosions, and they cast unnatural shadows throughout the building. I move toward the back where I know there are a few storage rooms; it seems like a probable place for Felix to hide.

I'm about to push open the door to one of the storage rooms when I hear Talina's voice coming from inside.

"This is ludicrous, Justin! We can't keep lying to them about what happened the other day."

"What are we supposed to do?" Justin exclaims. "Undermine the Governor? At this point I think the truth would only make the situation worse, plus we'd get ourselves an appointment with the Restrainers."

"But they're going to find out about the North sooner or later, and they need to be prepared for what's really coming! We're not doing them any favors by coddling them. In the end, it's just going to do more damage."

"How do we know the North wasn't just accidentally out of their jurisdiction? This is the first time they've made an assault beyond the Outer Reaches, maybe it was just a mistake."

"When has the North ever made a mistake?" Talina retorts.

"Look," Justin says, taking a deep breath, "I'm just saying that the Governor probably has a plan in place.

There's no need to get everyone worried until we're sure there's a real threat."

"I'd rather deal with worried trainees than completely unprepared trainees," Talina snaps. And before I have time to react, she opens the door and I'm staring her in the face.

"Dang it, Mari! Why is it always you?" She remarks. She looks me over, as if considering me, then shrugs her shoulders. "Well, at least one of you will have an idea of what's coming." And with that, she strides out of the nutrition hall. Justin steps out of the room and grabs me by the collar of my uniform.

"Don't you dare tell anyone what you heard, understand?" He threatens. He lets me go roughly and is gone before I have a chance to respond.

I let out a shaky breath and let myself lean on one of the tables close to me. *I knew it wasn't just a simulation!* And I agree with Talina, I think we all have a right to know what's really going on. Who is the North? The Outer Reaches? And what's coming? I make a mental note to ask Talina about it later, assuming I can talk to her in private anytime soon.

I hear a noise near the entrance of the hall and remember the reason I came here in the first place: to find Felix. I get up and walk toward the sound, hoping that it was him, but stop short when I see Jaren leaning against one of the still-crumbling doorways.

"Hey Mari," he says casually, as if we're on friendly terms, "I've been meaning to talk to you."

"What do you want, Jaren?" I answer back fiercely. I already hate him for whatever he did to Alia, plus I'm also on edge about the information I just overheard.

"Hey, calm down, girl," he chuckles. "I just wanted to say how impressed I was with what you did during the simulation. Quick thinking, very inspiring."

"Is that all?"

"Of course not, Mari," he says as he starts walking slowly toward me, "you are a remarkable girl and I would love to get to know you better."

Something about his tone makes me uneasy.

"What do you mean?" I ask steadily.

"Well," he gestures to the empty hall, "we're all alone and I can be very persuasive. Just ask your friend Alia. And about a dozen other girls," he adds with a twisted smile.

"Alia," I whisper to myself, starting to put the pieces together.

"Ah yes, Alia was fun for a while," Jaren says smugly. "I'm sorry to say that I got her into a bit of a predicament, but she worked it out. Turns out the Amplifier is good for getting rid of all kinds of ... mistakes."

The gravity of Alia's situation comes crashing down on me. The months of moodiness, the odd weight gain, her inconsolable sobbing the other night... I feel sick. Sick for not being there for her, sick for assuming she was just having petty boy problems, sick for this burden she's had to carry all alone. I start to shake in anger, but Jaren is still advancing.

"So, what do you say, Mari?" He oozes, "Nobody has to know. I'm sure you're curious, and then you'll at least have a pleasant memory from Training."

I want to strangle him. I want to scream profanities in his face and make him wish he'd never said a word to me. But instead, I will myself to be calm and take a step closer to him. I just have to pretend for a little while in order to inflict the most damage.

I force a coy smile and play with the edge of his sleeve.

"You know, Jaren," I simper, "I was actually a little jealous that Alia got to spend so much time with you."

"Really?" He murmurs as his eyes flash over my body, "Tell me more about that."

Ugh, he thinks he's actually going to get it. I swallow back revulsion.

"It's just that, I've been attracted to you for a while, and I was wondering if you were ever going to notice me," I mutter timidly.

I feel his lips on my neck and I almost lose it. *Just a few more seconds.*

"Well, Mari," he whispers in my ear, "tonight all of your dreams are going to come true."

Oh, if you only knew.

He puts his arms around my waist and pulls me close to him. Just as he starts to bring his lips to mine, I pull my knee up as hard as I can into his groin. He whimpers and collapses in pain, but I knee him in the groin several more times for good measure. Then I slam his head onto a nearby table and hiss into his ear.

160

"If you ever come near me or my friend again, I swear I will pulverize your manhood into oblivion."

I shove him onto the floor and run out of the nutrition hall while he moans in agony. I want to scour every inch of my skin, every place that he touched or breathed on or looked at. I'm just hoping I incapacitated him enough to keep him away from girls for a while. A long while.

I run all the way back to my dorm and I'm relieved to find Alia there alone. She's sitting on her bed staring at the wall. I rush forward and throw my arms around her.

"Mari, what happened to you?" She asks, clearly startled that I'm suddenly hugging her. "I waited for you in The Coliseum - "

"I know, Alia." I interrupt. "I ran into Jaren. I know about everything."

I feel her crumple into my embrace and soon her tears are soaking my shoulder.

"I didn't know what else to do," she confesses in between sobs, "and I didn't know how to tell you. I didn't know how to tell anyone." And suddenly she's telling me everything. The vulnerability, the confusion, the pain, and the loss. We cry together for a long time. And I realize that listening to her is far more effective means of support than pummeling her ex-boyfriend's private parts.

Chapter 24

The Restrainers arrived at 6:00 this morning. There were 20 of them, looking polished and ominous in their metallic uniforms. They did a short fighting demonstration for us and it was absolutely awe-inspiring. They were moving so fast it made me dizzy to watch them. Some of them were spinning and flipping so high up in the air they almost didn't seem like they were human. I'd love to become one of them. Too bad I've made such a bad impression with Governor Plenaris that that will never be a possibility. Afterwards, Talina and Justin lined us up alphabetically outside the Coliseum while the Restrainers filed in, and then they started calling trainees in 5 at a time to complete their assessment. Waiting is the worst part. It seems like it takes about 45 minutes for each group to go through the assessment, and I've been waiting for about 9 hours.

So far, not a single person has failed the assessment. At first, I was relieved when I saw that Alia had passed, but now I realize that I had nothing to worry about. I watch trainees that I know have done far less than Alia during Training emerge triumphantly from the Coliseum with completion certificates in their hands. I'm starting to wonder why we had to be here for three months if the final assessment was going to be so easy.

And then, of course, there's the whole issue of what the Restrainers will decide about my future. It may not even matter if I pass today if the Restrainers ultimately decide that I'm not fit to be Amplified. And then what will I do? I mean, I guess living without Amplification has worked out all right for my mom, but I don't know if I can settle for a life like hers. I don't know if I can be happy spending the rest of my life doing menial labor and being called a *clam*.

"Oh, Mari, you'll be fine without Amplification, there's already so much you can do on your own!"

That's what Alia said when I told her about my most recent meeting with Governor Plenaris and the impending decision of the Restrainers. I think she was just trying to be nice. Sure, I don't rely on my Amplifier as much as some other people do, but now that I've experienced it, I'd just feel so vulnerable and helpless without it. Not to mention the fact that I'd be severely inferior to 90 percent of the population.

Alia and I have spent a lot of time catching up over these past few days. She went into the particulars of her whole debacle with Jaren and disclosed a few things about the other trainees that she noticed when they thought she wasn't watching. Apparently she stumbled upon quite a few awkward moments. For my part, I finally told her about almost being strangled by the mysterious stranger in the hover chamber. She was horrified. I felt bad about making her worry so much, but a small part of me was glad that her fear somehow validated mine; that I wasn't overreacting. I still haven't told her anything about Felix or what I overheard the other night about the attack from the North. I don't want to inundate her with things to stress about.

Justin's gruff voice brings me out of my thoughts.

"Devon Nelson, Cassidy Prewitt, Tristan Prewitt, Marianna Quillen, and Joby Reams, please enter The Coliseum."

This is it, I think, but I'm not really nervous. More than anything I'm elated that I don't have to wait anymore. We follow Justin through the large doors of the Coliseum. Once inside, I see that the Restrainers are divided into 5 groups, one in each corner and one in the middle of the arena. Talina assigns each of us to a different group of Restrainers. I end up in the nearest corner by the wall of weapons.

I become increasingly intimidated as I approach the 4 Restrainers in the corner. They all narrow their eyes at me as I come near. Even though they all have vastly different physical attributes, somehow, they all look the same. One of them, a pale, thin man, steps forward and addresses me.

"Marianna Quillen, upon successful completion of this final assessment, your Training will be complete and you will become a formal soldier. You must pass through five tests to determine your skill and compliance with the Amplifier." He takes out a Transcriber. "This year you have the option of completing the tests on your own, or with the assistance of an Override." The man hands the Transcriber to me, and I take it gingerly. Now I know why no one has failed the assessment. It seems a little extreme. We just need to have the actions in our memory and know the right thing to say, but now we can forfeit those responsibilities too? I wonder just how many trainees opted for this route. Did Alia? I skim over the words. It appears to be a contract, but I don't read it too thoroughly because I already know what I'm going to choose.

"I'll complete the tests on my own," I announce confidently.

I see a hint of surprise flash through all the Restrainer's expressions before they make their faces indifferent again. Now I'm worried. Is the assessment so difficult that you need the help of an Override? Maybe this was a test to see how loyal I am to the Amplification system and I've already failed.

"Very well," the pale man finally responds. "We'll start with weapons."

Our small group moves in front of the wall of weapons, and one of the Restrainers flips up the training mode switch. I position myself in front of the first weapon, a crossbow, heft it out of its cradle, and obediently wait for the manikin to come out of the wall. When it does, I give myself a swift command, load the crossbow, take aim, shoot, and floor the dummy in less than 2 seconds.

I move down the line of weapons, giving myself commands and taking out the manikins. I'm careful when I reach the bow staff to only use the generic command. I have a little trouble trying to load the machine gun, but otherwise I make it through all the weapons without much trouble.

When I reach the end of the line, I turn and look back at all the defeated manikins. For a moment I imagine they're real bodies, and I feel a surge of horror course through me. But soon the cracks in the wall open up and pull the fake warriors back in, and I'm able to shake the feeling. The Restrainers are stoic as they take notes on their Transcribers. Eventually, they motion for me to follow them to the boxing ring.

I'm surprised when one of the Restrainers joins me in the ring, a short woman with graying hair and impressive curves. On a signal, we access our Amplifiers at the same time and start fighting. I can tell that she's intentionally holding back for my benefit; I know she's capable of far more than what she's doing. I guess they have no interest in keeping people from passing. I dodge a few of her punches and finally knock her down with a well-placed uppercut to her chin. Another one of the Restrainers comes in and resets her jaw, and then we move to the next test, calmly, as if I didn't just beat up one of my assessors.

The third test consists of retrieving a set of rings from various locations on the field. They're all pretty easy to get, except for the last one, which is suspended from the ceiling. I use the pole vault to launch myself into the air and reach it, but I overshoot it a little bit and am almost impaled by one of the ceiling's glass stalactites. I grab the ring on the way back down and land gracefully on the mat below.

I start to get uneasy when I see that we're heading next to the electrocution jungle. Maybe I *should* have opted for the Override. The pale man switches on the electricity and looks at me expectantly. Perhaps it's my hesitation that prompts him to explain the end goal.

"You are to make it to the other side and push the button without touching any of the cables."

I take a deep breath. I've never made it through the room and I've never seen anyone else do it. I guess I'll have to try to constantly give myself commands as I go through. I scan the jungle again, looking for a good place to start. I notice that the cables are more sparse near the ceiling, and every now and then I can see an exposed piece of pole. As far as I can recall, the poles aren't electrified. I guess there's only one way to find out.

"Mari, run up the wall and grab onto the nearest pole."

My body responds quickly, and before I know it I'm lunging off the top of the wall and reaching for the pole. I wince as my hands connect, bracing myself for a shock, but luckily, it doesn't come. I let my legs swing for half a second before I give myself another command.

"Mari, do a side aerial twist around the cables to the next pole."

My limbs contort through the buzzing wires as I spin and flip to reach the pole. The cables are becoming more dense and I need to think of my next move quickly. I look down and see a clear patch of floor.

"Mari, drop to the floor and roll to the left."

My shins burn slightly from the impact of such a long fall. I stand up gingerly to avoid contact with any of the cables, which is a difficult task since I'm surrounded by them. Apparently I've landed in the worst possible spot in the room. Everywhere I look I'm confronted by thick webs of dangerous wire. Unless some of the cables magically disappear, I have nowhere to go. But I can't just stay here, even if any move I make means I'll fail. Not to mention I'll have to endure those torturous shocks.

I choose the direction that I think takes me closer to the button. I dive straight into the cables and hope it's clear on the other side. Unfortunately, as I pass through the wall of chords, I'm cradled by more of the shock-inducing cables. I attempt to wriggle forward, but the jolts are so overwhelming that it's hard to move, much less concentrate on doing anything effective. With a fleeting moment of clarity, I give myself a last-ditch command.

"Mari, break one of the cables."

I scream out as my bare hands grab a cable in front of me. With every ounce of strength in my body, I rip the cable apart. Immediately, the electricity cuts out and I hang limply over the now-harmless cords. I can hear the Restrainers approaching, but I don't have the energy to lift my head.

"That was ... interesting," I hear a woman say flatly.

"Is she all right?" A man muses. "It'd be such a nuisance to have to deal with a dead body."

My disgust at their impassive comments fuels my adrenaline and I roll out of the cables and fall on my back onto the floor. There's a collective sigh from the Restrainers. I stare at them defiantly. One of them bends down and applies some sort of salve to my hands which soothes the burns.

"That was an impressive effort, Ms. Quillen," the pale man asserts, "however, you did not pass this particular test."

I don't know if it's my current fatigue or my overall declining respect for the Restrainers, but for some reason I break decorum and ask: "has *anyone* ever passed this test?"

There's a hint of a smile on the pale man's face. "No, actually," he states. "This test was designed to be impossible to achieve."

I stare at him for a few moments, wondering if he could possibly be making a joke.

"So then, why..."

"This room acts as a control to ensure that none of the Amplifiers are evolving," he explains.

My head is spinning. Do they expect the Amplifiers to evolve? And in what way? Independently of the person they're inhabiting? I want to ask him all of these things, but instead I ask the less pertinent question.

"So, this won't count against me for the assessment?"

"No," he says curtly, "it's merely a precautionary measure. Shall we move on?"

I follow the pale man and the other Restrainers to the urban obstacle course, but I'm still thinking about the possibility of my Amplifier taking on a mind of its own. Or perhaps stealing mine. Maybe this was part of what Talina meant when she warned about giving your Amplifier too much control of your mind. When we reach the course, the pale man turns around, points to the corner of the ceiling, and announces:

"There is something just beyond that pipe that doesn't belong here. You are to find it within 7 minutes and bring it back to us."

I swallow hard. He's pointing to the spot where I climbed up before and found Felix. Are they aware of the mysterious stowaway boy on the barge and do they know about our meeting? Is it Felix that I have to find and bring back down? Are they testing me to see if I'll volunteer information about him? Or is this just a nauseating coincidence?

I keep my expression smooth as I pass by the Restrainers and start up the course. If I do find Felix up there, I'm going to have to figure out a way to avoid turning him over to the Restrainers. But if they find out I protected him, I might be sent to prison. However, if I help them get Felix, then he could be sent to prison instead. Which is worse? Being confined and punished for the rest of your life or being riddled with the guilt of knowing you caused confinement and punishment for someone else?

I'm really starting to get dizzy with this moral dilemma as I run, jump, and climb through the course. Following the path I used before, I make it up to the pipe in just a few minutes. I shimmy up the pole and wedge myself through the ceiling, wincing at the thought of what I might see. But when my eyes adjust, there is no curly haired boy. Instead, I'm greeted by a small package with red numbers glowing in the dim light.

I've never been so glad to see a bomb in my life.

The numbers are counting down from one minute forty-seven seconds, apparently the time left until it detonates. I wonder briefly if I should bring it back to the Restrainers still active and let them defuse it, but I imagine all the things that could go wrong carting a live bomb back through the obstacle course and decide to take care of it now.

"Mari, deactivate the bomb."

My hands reach for the package and remove a panel in the front, exposing a dozen different wires. For a moment, I feel my brain stutter as the collection of wires appears unfamiliar, but then it recalculates and easily identifies the wires that need to be severed. I pull the designated wires out from the box a bit and cut them on a sharp edge of the air vent. The bomb emits a short, whining sound and the numbers on the bomb disappear.

I feel oddly unfulfilled knowing that all I contributed to this event was a few memories of pictures or films that I had seen before. The Amplifier did the rest. I guess I can't expect to feel rewarded when I hardly do any of the work. *Good job, Amplifier.* I make my way back down the course and present the defused bomb to the bored-looking group of Restrainers. The pale man makes a couple of notes on his Transcriber, then hands me a certificate.

"Congratulations, Miss Quillen."

Chapter 25

"I'm so glad it's over!" Alia shouts to me over the loud music.

"Yeah, me too," I shout back dutifully. But in all honesty, I don't know what to feel. My experience with the assessment was lackluster at best. I don't know if I'm going to get to stay Amplified and go on to Service with everyone else, and I have a nagging suspicion that things in the Community are about to change, and not for the better.

I look around the recreation lounge. It has been completely transformed for the concert. They brought in a rock group I've never heard of to perform in celebration of the end of our Training. Everybody else seems really psyched about it. I don't know why. I mean, I guess the band is good, but I'm pretty sure they're just using their Amplifiers.

On the other side of me, I hear Joby command himself to dance along with the music. I smirk as he moves somewhat unnaturally to the beat. I almost think he'd do a better job of it without the Amplifier.

It's hot and crowded and the music is starting to grate on my nerves. I'd much rather listen to the music on my device. I'm thinking I'll go back to my dorm room and do just that, when suddenly, I feel someone slide their hand around my waist. The encounter with Jaren is still fresh in my mind, so I'm not taking any chances. I snatch at the person's hand and twist it until its owner is brought to his knees.

"Dang, Mari, I guess there's no subtle way to make a move on you."

"Liam!" I gasp, helping him up from the floor, "I'm so sorry! I thought..." I trail off, not sure how to finish.

"You thought I was just some creep, huh? Well, next time I know to give you a fair warning."

"Maybe there shouldn't be a next time."

The words come out automatically, before I know I'm saying them. I'm not even sure that's how I wanted to respond. I'm definitely attracted to Liam, but for some reason I know getting romantically involved with him is a bad idea. Can't we just be friends?

Liam attempts a smile, but looks altogether unsure of himself.

"Okay, well, I'm gonna go find out what Todd is doing," Liam says lamely. "I guess I'll see you later, Mari."

I feel awful as I watch him walk away. I didn't want to hurt his feelings, but I see no point in leading him on. Alia is looking at me expectantly, but I don't know what to tell her.

"Why me?" I ask.

Alia opens her mouth to reply, but it's Joby's voice I hear behind me.

"It's your eyes."

I turn around and stare at him. My expression must be pretty severe because the smile fades from his face and he tries to backtrack.

"What I meant to say was that your eyes are unusually ... beautiful."

For the second time in three minutes words fail me. After a few uncomfortable moments, Alia cuts in.

"Hey Joby, do you want to go get some capsules with me?"

"Yes," Joby responds quickly, clearly grateful for a way out of this awkward situation. Alia gives me an amused grin.

"Who knew you'd turn out to be such a heartbreaker?" She whispers playfully as she slips by and heads off to the nutrition dispensers with Joby.

I exhale. Within a short amount of time I've managed to offend two of my very few friends. Thankfully, Alia was there to rescue me from my tactlessness. Once again she's shown how she has matured years since she's been here. She's far more intuitive and sensible than the girl I used to know.

I break away from the crowd listening to the band and find an empty couch to sit on. I don't really want to talk to anybody right now, I kind of feel like a social failure. *What is wrong with me?* Two pretty fantastic guys like me and I can't seem to conjure up genuine feelings for either one of them. Maybe I'm still too young for things like this, although somewhere deep down I know I have the capacity to have strong feelings for someone. The problem is, I don't know who it is.

I shake my head to try to get rid of my confusing thoughts. I notice a bowl of Intoxication capsules sitting on the table next to me. *Probably just another way to celebrate the end of Training*, I think as I pick up the bowl and study the brightly colored capsules. They really are mesmerizing, and despite my better judgement, my curiosity wins out. *Why not?* I rationalize, *Training is over and I'm probably going to go to bed soon anyway*. I pick out an orange and white capsule and pop it in my mouth.

The flavor is tangy and sweet and I immediately feel myself relax, despite the mild anxiety I was experiencing just a moment ago. I notice a tiny bit of haziness in my otherwise clear mind. I decide to test my Amplifier to see if it really has shut off.

"Mari, do ten push ups."

Nothing happens. My body doesn't respond; I feel none of the familiar urges to complete the command. It's freeing, in a way. This is the first time my Amplifier has not worked, and for some reason it makes me laugh.

"Hi Mari!"

My laugh turns into a scream as Cassidy jumps onto the couch next to me and the bowl of Intoxication capsules launches into the air. She really has an uncanny way of startling people. She looks worried, so I try to recover quickly.

"Sorry, Cassidy, I guess I'm just a little jumpy tonight," I explain.

"Oh, don't worry! I'm jumpy all the time!" She responds. "Here, I'll help you clean these up," she offers as she starts to collect the scattered capsules. I join her.

"Where's your brother?" I ask nonchalantly, not really sure if I care.

"Oh, he's with Talina getting his mistake fixed."

I really want to ask what his mistake was, but I feel like it would be impolite to pry. Turns out there's no need, though, because Cassidy plows right on.

"That idiot tried to command himself to solve all his problems, but instead he commanded himself to solve all *the* problems."

"Really?"

"Yeah, and he's been spending hours obsessively working out every problem he encounters."

I look at Cassidy for a moment, and then we burst out laughing. I mean, it's really not that funny; it would be exhausting to constantly have to be working out mathematical equations and ethical dilemmas, not to mention scientific incongruences and who knows what else, but it is a little comedic that such a small mistake caused such a personal disaster. If I didn't hate him so much I'd feel sorry for him. We pick up the last of the spilled capsules and sit back on the couch.

"So what did you think of the assessment?" Cassidy asks.

"It wasn't too bad," I answer. "It was a little weird, though."

"I know!" Cassidy nearly shouts. "The new offer with the Override really threw me off! I almost went for it, because I was so nervous, but then I read the contract and decided to do it on my own."

"What did it say?" I ask, wishing I had read through it more thoroughly.

Cassidy's face becomes somber. "There was a lot of normal, mundane stuff, but at the end, it said if we chose to use the Override for the assessment, we would be subject to perform other various assignments conducted by the Override."

I shiver. "You mean people can be overridden at random without an emergency?"

"That's what it sounds like."

Uneasiness creeps through me. How many of the trainees decided to use the Override for their test? Did they know by doing so that they could be used at any time as pawns for whatever the Community deems necessary?

"Anyway," Cassidy blurts out, suddenly shedding all her seriousness, "I'm going to go see if I can get the band to autograph my arm!"

I watch her gallop off toward the stage, her white-blonde hair nearly glowing in the new lights they put in for the concert. I consider her for a moment. Maybe she's exaggerating what the contract actually said. She does seem the type to get a little paranoid about things like this. Although, if her interpretation really was correct, I can't imagine the Community would use people for anything too serious. They'll probably just use them for routine tasks and tests.

Now that I've rationalized away most of my anxiety about the Override, I let my mind wander back to my most recent encounter with Governor Plenaris. I wonder if there's any way I can persuade him to allow me to stay Amplified. He didn't say anything definitive when we last spoke, and I was surprised that he remained calm during my outburst. Although, that might just be the way he reacts to everything. Maybe the Restrainers will be merciful. I'm only a 15-year old girl, after all. Maybe they won't see me as such a threat.

It just seems that now, more than ever, it's important to have the advantage of the Amplifier. Something big is coming, and I want to be equipped with the best defenses when it does. The fact that we've never heard of this mysterious North and that the Governor was so obsessed with covering up their attack tells me that our fantastic Community isn't as ideal or as stable as I've always thought. Tonight, if I can find her, and if she'll let me ask, I want to find out more about the North from Talina.

My head is starting to hurt and I realize it's getting pretty late. If I'm going to track down Talina, I better start looking now. I stand up and stretch to fend off some of my fatigue, then turn around just in time to see Joby's face before he punches me hard in the stomach.

"Hey!" I cry out in alarm. "Look, Joby, I'm sorry if I hurt your feelings, but do you really think this is the best way to handle-" I stop short when I see Joby's face. He looks absolutely terrified.

"Mari, I'm so sorry!" He says pathetically as he takes another swing at my face. I duck just in time.

"Joby, what's happening?"

"It's the Override!"

Now it's my turn to be terrified. All of Cassidy's words about the contract come flooding back into my brain. Of course Joby would have chosen to be overridden for the assessment, and now he's dealing with the twisted consequences. And apparently, so am I.

Joby comes at me with a spinning kick. I try to get past him, but his foot connects hard with my thigh and I fall to the ground.

"Joby, whose voice are you hearing?" I yell at him. "Is it Talena? Justin?"

"No!" He responds desperately, "It's neither of them!"

He lunges at me and I roll out of the way.

"Then who is it?"

"I don't know, but it sounds kind of like — "

Immediately, his mouth slams shut. Naturally, whoever is conducting this Override is not going to let him tell me who they are. But I have a pretty good idea. I try to get up, but Joby slams me to the ground and puts his arm across my throat, cutting off all my air. I struggle to free myself, but the weight of his body is too much. His face is inches from mine, his eyes are filled with tears.

All at once, Joby goes limp. I see a pair of hands roll him off of me, and look up to see Alia with a tranquilizer gun in her hand.

Chapter 26

"Mari, are you all right?" Alia asks, rushing to help me up. "I don't know what happened! One minute I'm talking to Joby, and the next minute he starts acting really weird and runs off."

"Where'd you get the gun?" I ask her wearily.

"Oh, I've just started keeping one with me since Jaren..." She answers a little sheepishly.

"Well, I'm glad you had it. I think you just saved my life."

"Mari, I had no idea Joby was going to come after you like that! It's not like him at all!"

"It wasn't him, it was the Override."

"What are you talking about?"

But I don't have time to explain. Behind Alia, I see about 2 dozen trainees coming toward me. Now I know exactly how many opted for the Override during the assessment and are now subject to performing a "random assignment." Most of them are looking at me with fear and confusion, and a few are wearing an expression of demonic delight. One of these is Jaren, and I notice with a fleeting moment of satisfaction that he's walking awkwardly. *Guess he hasn't recovered yet.* I start to think of a command to give myself, but then remember with a sinking realization that the Intoxication I ate has rendered my Amplifier useless.

"Mari, what is going on?" Alia asks shakily, watching the small army of trainees approaching.

"I need your tranquilizer gun," I say urgently.

Before Alia has time to respond, I wrench the gun out of her hands and start shooting at my overridden attackers. My aim is a little off without the Amplifier, but I see about 7 of them drop to the floor before I run out of darts. I thrust the gun back at Alia and run straight through the pack toward the stage. They seem to hesitate for a moment, but then turn and start to run after me.

I leap onto the stage, vaguely hearing cries of protest from the band, which turn into cries of fear when my pursuers follow suit. I knock over the drum set, and a few of the trainees stumble over it. An unusually tall boy is right on my heels, but I grab a bass guitar and smash it into his face. He topples backwards and takes down two other trainees that were behind him. Their numbers are dwindling, but there's still a dangerous amount of trainees that are trying to kill me.

I jump off the stage and run hard to the other side of the recreation lounge, toward the middle of the aerial obstacle course. I don't dare look back because I don't want to lose any speed, but I can hear their feet pounding close behind me. Praying that my plan works, I jump over the barricades and straight into the hole in the floor that makes up the second half of the Plunge. All of my attackers follow me, so I'm hoping this means the air turbines are going to turn on and stop us from falling hundreds of feet to our death. Otherwise, whoever is orchestrating this Override has just mercilessly killed about a dozen teenagers.

In the split-seconds of my free fall, I vaguely remember some old anecdote about sheep jumping off a cliff. *How did that go?* Thankfully, I don't have time to figure it out because the air turbines gear up and nearly knock the wind out of me. We collectively shoot back up through the hole in the floor and I start hitting and kicking whoever is closest to me as best as I can in mid air. I manage to knock a couple of girls unconscious before the turbines shut off and we're all falling back into the hole in the floor.

On the way down, someone kicks me in the back, sending me crashing into a boy just below me. He twists to face me and starts to strangle me, but he loses his grip when the air turbines come back on. I head butt him and push him away from me, but grab his legs when we emerge from the hole again. Swinging the boy around by his feet, I'm able to knock a few others away from me. There are several unconscious people now, bobbing around in the air and falling lazily with each cycle of the turbines. Seems like the person in charge of the Override is getting confused by all of this motion because some of the trainees are attacking each other. Regardless, I'm still very vulnerable and getting pretty beat up. I need to find a way out of the Plunge.

We fall through the hole once again, but this time I try to position myself close to the edge. When the turbines shoot us up again, I use all my strength to propel myself out of the air stream, but I don't get myself out nearly as fast as I wanted, so I still fall about 10 feet to the floor outside of the hole. My knees buckle as I hit the ground and roll several feet away from the Plunge. I try to get up and run, but my body aches so much that all I can manage is to get onto my hands and knees.

My hair has fallen over my face, and through the dark red strands I can see the rest of my assailants exiting the air stream, some more successfully than others, and advancing toward me. I groan. I don't think I have any energy left to fight. And what's more, I see 6 of the other overridden trainees that didn't follow me into the Plunge approaching from the other side. *This is the end*, I think. *I'm going to be beaten to death by my own peers.*

I use the last of my will power to stand up. If nothing else, I'm not going to die on my hands and knees. I push my hair out of my face and watch the trainees closing in on me, some still with sheer panic in their eyes. *It's all right, I'm going to see my dad soon.*

But then, the lights start flashing and a siren goes off. Through the wail of the siren, we hear this announcement:

"Attention, the air barge is under attack. All capable trainees and other Amplified individuals will be subject to the Override to combat the assault. The Override will begin in 10 seconds."

In the momentary reprieve between Overrides, a few of my previously deadly attackers rush forward and apologize. Even though they just almost killed me, I feel sorry for them. Through my numbness, I try to summon up what it would feel like to be forced to try to kill someone else, much less someone you consider to be a friend. I look beyond them and see Jaren looking sour, he really must have wanted to kill me. Next to him is Aaron, the boy I bested in the hover chamber. He looks angry, but not at me. He may not be my biggest fan, but I bet that he's more bothered by the Override than by not having the chance to finish beating me up.

Then all at once, everyone around me becomes rigid and runs in unison out of the recreation lounge. The massive room clears as even the members of the band fall in line and rush outside. I only see a few people left; some that are unconscious on the floor and a few that are wandering helplessly around. They must have taken Intoxication, like me.

I limp outside to see where the Override is taking everybody. About 100 feet away I see the trainees pouring out of a building carrying guns and other various weapons. It must be an armory. I watch as everyone lines up on the North side of the barge, their weapons at the ready. For a few endless minutes there is complete silence. And then they come.

They fall from the sky and spill over the south and west sides of the barge. There are hundreds of them, wearing heavy black vests and helmets that completely cover their faces, each toting a massive gun. Somehow, I know exactly who they are, and they're not the North. Despite everything the Community did to make them seem ridiculous, it's clear that these people are a legitimate threat.

These are the Dissenters.

Chapter 27

Everything happens at once. The Dissenters open fire. I want the trainees to retreat, to flee — they are clearly outnumbered, but they don't. They are powerless against the will of the Override. My peers return fire, but their bullets, darts and arrows hardly penetrate the heavy protective armor of the Dissenters. I watch a few trainees go down in front and I scream. *So much for staying out of the action.* My scream alerts a few Dissenters and one of them breaks away and starts coming toward me. From their build, I'm guessing it's a man.

I'm still exhausted from being attacked by the overridden trainees, but somewhere inside me I find adrenaline and burst into a run. The Dissenter doesn't shoot at me, thankfully, but he is quickly gaining speed. I glance back and notice that the Dissenters have broken ranks and are splitting up. I can't imagine it's because we're winning, but it gives me hope that maybe something is going well for my peers.

I run to the Coliseum, nearly smashing into the massive doors as I try to escape my pursuant. Unfortunately, he's only about 20 feet behind me. *Why doesn't he just shoot me and put me out of my misery?* I think. Not that I'm eager to die, I'm just wondering about his tactics. Maybe he's one of those deranged types that likes to tear their prey apart with their bare hands. That disturbing image gives me a jolt of energy and I sprint forward.

I go straight to the wall of weapons and activate the training mode. Running along the wall, I pull off as many weapons as I can, and grab a small pistol to keep with me. I can hear the cracks in the walls opening and the manikins coming out, assaulting the Dissenter behind me. I turn around to check if my plan is working and I'm stopped dead in my tracks by what I see.

The Dissenter is taking on about 7 manikins at once, but he clearly has the upper hand. He's dodging arrows and knives by hitting, spinning, and kicking, all the while pitting the dummies against each other. He moves with more speed and agility than anyone I've ever seen, even the Restrainers. I nearly choke as I watch him flip over and rip the arms off of one of the manikins.

Who is this guy? Is it possible that a portion of the Dissenters have some sort of Amplification? Although, it seems he's using moves different from the ones programmed in the Amplifiers. Even now, he runs up the front of a manikin, wraps his legs around its head, and twists it down to the ground. The last two manikins shoot at each other until rendered lifeless. The Dissenter brushes himself off and turns his attention back to me.

Great, I think, *I've been idiotically standing here in awe of my enemy when I could have been getting away.* I take off across the Coliseum and fire back a few ineffective shots with the pistol. At least I've had a bit of a rest, while he's visibly drained from fending off the manikins. I head straight to the electrocution room, quickly shut off the electricity, and plunge into the maze of cables. I smile with satisfaction when I hear the

Dissenter follow me in. I loop around the back of the room and then run out to turn the electricity back on.

The effect is immediate. The cables buzz to life and the Dissenter yells out in surprise and pain. It looks like he's caught near the back of the room, where the cables are swinging as he struggles to free himself from the agonizing shocks. He grunts a few times, and then suddenly I hear an odd thump and the cables start to retract into the ceiling. As the cords lift, I see a boot on the floor below the button and the Dissenter hobbling back to retrieve it. *Of course*, I think bitterly, *my pursuer is the one person to outsmart this room.*

But even more shocking is that the back wall is opening up to reveal row after row of shiny, silver Override machines. My mind starts racing. Why would they be storing dozens of Override machines on the training barge? Did Justin really want to see us succeed in this electrocution room or did he have ulterior motives? Did the Restrainers test all of us in here as a control experiment or to ensure that these machines were still safe?

The Dissenter takes a few steps toward the machines, apparently he's forgotten about me for the moment. He reaches into his vest and pulls out a Transmitter. I assume he's about to alert the rest of his Dissenter buddies about the Override machines. Suddenly, I'm filled with a sense of urgency. If the Dissenters get a hold of these machines, we are all screwed. The entirety of our Amplified Community will be at the mercy of these crazed rebels. I go from victim to attacker. I don't know what I'm doing — my Amplifier is still useless, but I just know I have to keep the Dissenters away from those Override machines.

My only advantage is that he doesn't see me coming. I run at him with all of my might and slam into his back before he's able to speak into the Transmitter. We fall to the floor and I try to hold him down by shoving my knee into his back, but he shakes me off easily. Before I know it, he's on top of me and poised to punch me senseless, but for some reason, he freezes.

"Mari Quillen?"

His voice. It's *the* voice. The mysterious voice from the recording on my device. I struggle to free one of my hands and hurriedly pull off his helmet.

And suddenly I'm staring into the honey-brown eyes of Miles Paxton.

Chapter 28

The words come quickly and from both sides. We shout over each other in a jumble of confused excitement.

"Where have you been?"

"Why didn't you try to find me?"

"What are you doing here?"

"Did you get my message?"

"When did you join the Dissenters?"

"Are you still Amplified?"

"Why did you leave me?"

My last question silences Miles. He looks caught off guard and stares at me inquisitively. I take in his features. He is absolutely striking. He has the same smooth, tan skin and thick black hair that I remember, and the past three years have sharpened the angles of his face. His eyes are so intense, yet softened somehow by their honey-tinged color. I feel my pulse quickening. Seeing his face again brings back all the memories, all the feelings of betrayal.

"Why did you leave me?" I repeat, getting up from the ground with some difficulty. "You were my only friend, and you just disappeared! I didn't even know if you were still alive! And right after my father had died —"

"I lost my entire family!" Miles explodes, jumping to his feet. "I didn't trust the Community and I didn't want to be part of it anymore!"

I exhale as I remember that Miles' father, mother, and older sister all died of the 12-hours virus. His neighbors had taken him in after that, but he never seemed to recover from the loss.

"Mari," Miles continues, "I'm sorry. But I thought you would follow me."

"Follow you where? You never told me where you were going!"

"I didn't *know* where I was going!" He retorts. "I just thought you'd be smart enough..."

"Smart enough to what? Run off into the desert and magically stumble into you? Leave behind my family and the chance to be Amplified?"

"The chance to be Amplified?" Miles spits out in disgust. "So that's what it comes down to? You chose Amplification over me?"

"I didn't know there was an ultimatum," I fire back.

"And what has Amplification done for you, Mari? It's just held you back and put you under the scrutiny of Governor Plenaris."

"How did you — "

"We're tapped into the Community's surveillance system," Miles explains. "I've been watching you since I left."

I should feel violated and a little creeped out. So why do my cheeks flush with pleasure?

"Plus Felix has been keeping us updated," Miles states.

"Felix?"

"Yeah, he's our spy. Smart kid." Miles chuckles. "He's a big fan of yours. He was supposed to get everyone on the air barge Intoxicated before we got here, but it seems like there was a snag."

Yeah, I think, *a bunch of trainees were trying to kill me.*

"So that was your big plan?" I ask sarcastically, "To render everyone useless so you could come up here and slaughter us?"

"It's an effective plan," Miles responds. "How do you think I got past the guards at the nutrition factory?"

Of course. So simple, yet brilliant. Like throwing your shoe at a button to avoid being electrified.

"Plus, we didn't come up here to kill you guys. See?" He holds up his huge weapon, and I can see it's only a tranquilizer gun. I look down at my pistol and feel a twinge of guilt as I remember that a few minutes ago I was trying to kill Miles. Well, before I knew it was Miles.

"So what did you come here to do?" I ask.

"We came to find these," Miles replies, gesturing toward the Override machines.

"Oh great, so we'll all be subject to the demented whims of the Dissenters," I remark harshly.

Miles frowns at me. Probably because I've just inadvertently insulted him. I guess I still can't wrap my mind around the fact that Miles is a Dissenter.

"No," Miles says slowly, "we want to destroy them." The confusion must show on my face, because he continues his explanation. "It's bad enough that the

Amplified can be overridden by the Community, but if these machines were to be overtaken by someone else, it would be disastrous. You'd have an instant army at your disposal. The potential damage would be devastating. I can't even imagine what would happen if the North got their hands on these..."

"You know about the North?" I interrupt.

"Of course. Haven't they told you?"

"They've intentionally kept the North a secret," I respond. "Who are they?"

"Mari, there is so much outside of the Community," Miles says gravely. "There are other cities and communities, and the North is probably the most threatening. If they gain control, it's gonna be hell for the rest of us."

My head reels as I attempt to process this new and life-altering information. *What's beyond the Community? How many other people are there?*

"I talked to your mom about it briefly when she was hiding me at the farm. We're trying to come up with a plan."

I snap out of my thoughts. "You talked to my *mom?*" I ask, nearly delirious with confusion. But then I remember what my mom had mentioned in the Adhesive and I'm filled with anger.

"You! The Restrainers were looking for *you!*" I fume. "What would they have done to my mom, to Daniel, if they had found you? What on earth were you doing there that could possibly justify putting my family in so much danger?"

"Calm down, Mari!" Miles yells at me. "I was just getting some seeds and machinery designs. But mostly, I was there to find out about you!"

I'm lost for words. I know I'm blushing again and I wish more than anything that I wasn't. I'm angry that he left in the first place and that he's now a Dissenter, but underneath all that, I'm elated to see him again. I should tell him. I should let him know how much I missed him, but I can't bring myself to say it.

"Mari," Miles says gently as he moves a few steps closer, "I had to fight. I had to leave. But you have filled my thoughts every single day since then."

My breath catches. All of my other concerns and anxieties slip away as I take him in. He closes the small gap between us and I try to lean in, but I can't, because suddenly I hear a faint voice in my head and my body stiffens.

"Mari, kill him."

I'm not at all surprised that it's the Governor's voice I hear coming through the Override. The Intoxication I took must be wearing off. I take a step back and look up at Miles in alarm. He's the last person on earth I want to kill right now.

"Are you okay?" Miles asks, clearly concerned. My hand automatically lifts the pistol and before I know it I'm aiming at Miles' head.

"Run," I whisper shakily.

"Mari, what are you doing?" Miles demands.

"Run!" I yell at him. I concentrate all my self control on not pulling the trigger, but still Miles doesn't

193

move. The voice comes into my head again, more powerful this time.

"Mari, kill him!"

My hand is trembling and I'm sweating from the effort of resisting the command.

"Miles, get out of here!"

My resolve is momentarily weakened from screaming at Miles, and I pull the trigger, but I'm able to shift my aim slightly downwards before I do. The bullet hits his shoulder and knocks him to the floor, but thanks to his heavy vest, it doesn't penetrate. He stands and gives me a desperate look, but finally exits the room.

My body starts to run after him, still trying to complete the command, but I manage to throw myself on the ground. My body writhes and I fire off a few shots in the direction Miles went, but he's safely out of range.

I have to figure out a way to make the command impossible to complete, I think. Every muscle is straining against the urge to stand up and follow Miles. I scream in agony as I twist around and shoot the rest of the bullets at the rows of Override machines.

My body relaxes and a few of the machines explode. Looks like I helped the Dissenters out a little bit after all. I'm completely exhausted and I can only imagine the damage that's been done elsewhere on the barge. But what drains me the most is the thought that I may never see Miles again.

Chapter 29

I'm really starting to hate these chairs. Almost as much as I hate these patronizing and intimate meetings with Governor Plenaris. I've been sitting here alone in the control room for about 20 minutes, waiting for the Governor and whoever else is invited to this exclusive conference to show up. I feel too restless to be stuck by myself in a small room.

A few minutes after Miles left, one of the Restrainers found me in the Coliseum and escorted me over to the control room, explaining that Governor Plenaris wanted to meet with me. I was able to draw a little information out of the stoic Restrainer on the way to the control room, mainly that the Dissenters escaped with a few override machines, and that while there were numerous injuries, no one was killed. It was a little eerie walking across the barge. Even though I knew they were only unconscious, it was jarring to see dozens of trainees lying wide-eyed and lifeless on the ground. It looked like the Dissenters tranquilized almost everyone. I wonder why they left so quickly when there was almost no resistance.

And now I'm in here alone with nothing to distract me from my thoughts of Miles. Remembering our encounter makes me ache in a way I'm altogether unfamiliar with. It's an ache that I never want to feel again and at the same time I don't want it to go away. Before tonight, I believed my behavior and choices just affected me, but now I feel peculiarly linked to Miles and

I'm suddenly terribly anxious to know the outcome of the Restrainers' decision concerning my future. I don't even know what I want their decision to be, I just want to be able to move forward. Why did Miles have to join the Dissenters? If he would have just stayed and become Amplified things could be so different right now.

And yet, the way Miles looked at me before he fled still haunts me. It was as if my actions were the ultimate betrayal. I mean, sure, I was shooting at him, but he has to understand how hard it was for me to try to resist the command to kill him. Would he understand? I don't know if I'll ever have the chance to explain it to him.

I need a distraction. I stand up and go over to the panel that controls the screens. At random, I push a few buttons and the room lights up with a dull, blue glow. I shiver as I look at all the images of still unconscious trainees strewn across the deck of the barge. I press a few more buttons and suddenly I'm watching Todd and Hannah kissing in one of the dorms. Immediately uncomfortable, I frantically run my fingers across the panel, willing the screens to show something else. The surveillance changes and I'm now viewing Governor Plenaris in the electrocution room with some of the Restrainers. They're gesturing to the override machines and I strain to hear what they're saying.

"He was in here, why didn't he take them?" A wiry Restrainer comments. The "he" must be Miles. So much for trying to distract myself.

"I found the Quillen girl here a few minutes later, she must have held him off." I recognize the Restrainer that took me to the control room.

"The Override held him off, and the command was not executed very well through the Quillen girl," Governor Plenaris responds blandly.

"But he could have alerted the others..."

"No," the Governor interjects, "when I threatened to kill the trainees, the Dissenters fled. There wouldn't have been time."

All the Restrainers nod in understanding. Not a single one of them seems at all shocked or indignant about the potential slaughtering of the trainees, of hundreds of members of the Community. Maybe it was an empty threat; a scare tactic to get the Dissenters to leave. Regardless, I feel sick.

"Fortunately, only a few of the machines were taken, but they got far too close this time," Governor Plenaris states. Only a slight furrow of his brow interrupts his normally glassy expression. "We'll have to find out where they're getting their supplies from. They need to be cut off."

There is an odd moment of silence as the Restrainers look at Governor Plenaris, but none of them meet his eye. It's almost as if they feel guilty for the current situation. He breaks the silence.

"Well, we have one last thing to take care of," the Governor announces, almost cheerfully. "Shall we adjourn to the control room?"

I gulp. I'm assuming that last thing is me, but the way he says, "take care of" nearly sounds like, "get rid of." I watch the group head out of the Coliseum and quickly move to shut off all the screens. I wouldn't want them knowing that I was spying on them. Although, considering their resources, they probably already know. A few minutes later I hear them coming down the stairs, their footsteps sounding as metallic as their uniforms.

Governor Plenaris comes into view first, and I stand to acknowledge him. The Restrainers file in behind, followed by Talina, Justin, and a large, blonde man I don't recognize.

"Have a seat, Miss Quillen," the Governor recites automatically, but I remain standing. For a moment, it appears Governor Plenaris doesn't mind, but then he presses a small, silver band on his wrist and suddenly I hear his voice in my head again.

"Mari, sit down."

My body clumsily falls into the chair behind me. I'm filled with rage as I realize that my previous fear is confirmed: The Governor has a personal Override machine that he can employ with only his thoughts. And I suppose the Override rules don't apply to him either; he can override someone whenever he wants, with or without an emergency. Doesn't seem very conducive to the Equality Movement to me.

I study The Governor and all of his flaws jump out at me. One of his eyebrows is bigger than the other. His earlobes hang down too much. The color of his skin looks fake. And of course there's his awful, shrill voice that he accosts me with now.

"As you may have gathered, Miss Quillen, the Restrainers and I have spent a considerable amount of time analyzing your decorum over the past few months. Please understand that we do not treat these matters lightly."

Oh, just get it over with! I think. *Either you're taking away my Amplification or you're sending me to prison! Stop wasting my time with all your formal statements!*

"After extensive deliberation, we have decided to make you a Restrainer."

My jaw drops. I glance at the others, looking for some sign that this is a cruel joke, but they all look nonplussed; they knew this was going to happen. I expected a lot of different outcomes, but this is beyond any possible situation I might have imagined. Not only am I spared from prison, but I get to stay Amplified *and* become a Restrainer? I get to have enhanced Amplification? This is fantastic, but it just doesn't add up.

"The Restrainers and I agreed that your skills and temperament would be best suited in serving the Community at maximum Amplification," the Governor continues. He gestures to the blonde man on his right. "Evan has agreed to be your personal mentor for the transition."

I inhale sharply when I hear the name. I look at the man more closely and see that a patch of his blonde hair is missing from the side of his head.

"He tried to strangle me!" I blurt out, suddenly aware that I've startled everyone in the room. "He almost killed me in the hover chamber!"

"Yes, that was a test," Governor Plenaris replies smoothly. "It was an evaluation of how you would handle such a situation. Similarly, you were being tested when you were attacked by your peers earlier tonight. You performed marvelously. We would not have let them kill you."

I open my mouth to respond, but I can't find words to convey my scattered thoughts. Taking my silence as acceptance, the Governor resumes his speech.

"Because you will become the youngest individual ever to be appointed to the Restrainer position, certain precautions must be taken to ensure compliance with the Equality Movement."

He keeps on talking, but I can't concentrate on what he's saying. I have too many fragments of events and ideas floating around in my brain, fighting for attention and order. The Governor has lied before, how do I know he's not lying now? Can I be certain that these attempts to end my life were really just tests? Or did he decide that if he can't kill me, he'll just have to keep me as close to him as possible by making me a Restrainer? Is this his way of discreetly controlling me? Of slowly killing my spirit? Plus, he knows I'm somehow connected to Miles, is he going to try to use me to infiltrate the Dissenters?

The euphoria and relief I felt a moment ago gives way to a sickening, sinking feeling. I can't trade my self will for flattery and an attractive position. I can't trust the Governor, the Restrainers, or the Community. Suddenly everything I ever thought I wanted is slipping out of my reach, and by my choice. Things have changed. I have changed. To accept the Restrainer position would be to give in to the Governor's system of control. And I don't give in.

There's only one way out of this.

I turn my focus back to Governor Plenaris. He's still rambling on about the details of my transition.

"Take it out," I say quietly.

The Governor pauses, cocking his head slightly to the side.

"What was that, Miss Quillen?"

I lift my head, look him in the eye, and emphasize every word.

"Take. It. Out."

Something flashes in The Governor's eyes. Was it fear?

"I don't understand what you mean, Miss Quillen," he says evenly. "You'll have to be a little more clear." He knows exactly what I mean. But if he wants me to spell it out for everyone so there can be no mistake, so be it.

"I choose to have my Amplifier removed," I announce.

Everyone else in the room stirs uncomfortably. I hear a few murmurs of surprise and shock. I glance over at Talina. She's smiling. The Governor clears his throat and the room becomes silent again. He studies me for a moment, as if weighing his options. But he must know that he can't deny me this choice.

"Very well," he finally responds.

For a moment I'm unsure what to do. Should I just go back to the Implantation Building and wait for an administrator to come take out my Amplifier? I don't have to wonder for long. For the third time tonight, the Governor's voice invades my thoughts.

"Mari, remove your Amplifier."

I look up in horror. The Governor returns my stare with an almost sadistic expression. I understand in an instant. This is his last chance to control me, he's not going to pass that up. My loathing for this man has just increased exponentially. To force me to operate on myself with nothing but my bare hands is truly evil. This is the man behind our "brilliant" Community.

My fingers claw at the site behind my ear where the Amplifier is embedded. I feel blood running down my neck and I want to scream, but I refuse to let the Governor know how much pain I'm experiencing. My body starts to spasm as I dig deeper into my tissue. His Override is trying to get me to tear out the Amplifier, but I know that if I don't disable it first, the still-attached tentacles will damage my nerves and I'll probably die. My tears are flowing freely, but I still don't make a sound. With my last remaining shred of resolve, I stall the command of the Override and crush the flat base of my Amplifier with my fingers. I feel a slight release of pressure in my neck as the tentacles go limp. Of my own volition, I pull out the lifeless Amplifier.

Then everything goes black.

————-

When I wake up, I'm in my room back at my compound. My head is aching. It's hot, and my skin sticks to the sheets on my bed. My mother is standing over me, smiling.

"Welcome back, Mari."

Printed in Great Britain
by Amazon